EVENING TRAIL
A Southern Tale

A SOUTHERN TALE

Evening Trail

MARTHA C.

Doris, You have always
been an encouragement to
me to travel, learn about
birds and do the things that
I want to do. This book is
is a true testimonial
that we can all achieve
our goals! ♡ CC Britt

LUMINARE PRESS
WWW.LUMINAREPRESS.COM

Cover Design: Melissa K. Thomas
Luminare Press
442 Charnelton St.
Eugene, OR 97401
www.luminarepress.com

LCCN: 2019904419
ISBN: 978-1-64388-114-0

Dedicated to my husband and the hunting
friends who never go away.

"He was a mighty hunter before the Lord."
(Genesis 10:9)

Author's Note

May 14, 2001

ONLY A DIM LIGHT FALLS THROUGH THE STAINED glass. Outside a storm threatens and churns; inside the church, the air is stuffy but calm. Mother and I slide into a pew near the center of the nave, where we have a clear view of everyone in the church. This is a historic building—an American gothic church built in the 1800s with dark weathered wood and crimson shutters, and it's one of the few buildings around town that was spared when most everything else was burned down in the Civil War. All this made the place feel especially ominous on a day like today. Funerals, especially for someone like Mrs. Leigh, are one of those events I always knew would come sooner rather than later, but always hoped never would. Mrs. Virginia Leigh was one of the most wonderful people I've ever met. She and her late husband, Mr. Andrew Leigh, were both special, and not a day goes by I'm not thankful for knowing them. Howard, my husband, feels the same but didn't come with me because he said he had something to take care of. I wondered if there wasn't more to his refusal, but I didn't press and came with Mother instead.

"I hope the weather doesn't interfere with the boat ride later," Mother says as the gusting wind slams closed the door.

"Maybe it will clear up," I say, as hopeful as possible that something like the weather doesn't interfere with Mrs. Leigh's final wishes. The funeral procession will take her by boat across the river to where she'll be buried on Horne Island, which was, until recently, privately owned by the Leigh family. The Leighs stayed four or five months a year in Riverside Village, but kept a full-time staff of six people over there all year round. Tony was the property manager, Roy the groundskeeper, Doug the gardener, Wilma (Roy's mother) cleaned, Frannie cooked, Toot fed the animals, and they all lived over there. All that's changed now. Growing up in Riverside Village, I spent a lot of time on Horne Island. We fished in the ponds and walked through the woods. I remember a line of tall palm trees standing in a perfect line, marking where a road used to lead to a house that isn't there anymore. And then in 1976 I married Howard, a skilled marksman and hunter who started helping on Horne when he became friends with Tony. Tony and his wife, PJ, had a daughter about the same age as ours, and we've been close ever since. We'd all spent so much time hunting on Horne that, at the end of the day, we'd put the horses on the trail we always took back to the house, and they'd drive themselves all the way. We called it the Evening Trail, because every evening, that's the one we took home. Even the horses knew.

I started doing Mrs. Leigh's hair when they came into town from New York—always the same page-boy cut, parted on the side and curled under just so and then pinned back with combs on the sides. I cut Mr. Leigh's hair too, every time they came to town. They used to beg me to go to New York and live with them, and I'd say, "Mr. Leigh, I can't go to New York." The Leighs kept an apartment in Manhattan and also owned another island in New York. But they

Martha C.

loved Riverside Village and spent every winter hunting in the dove fields—Riverside Village's finest, Mr. Leigh always said. Spending so much time out there, we all became very good friends. Although I hope the friendships last forever, today might be my last boat ride to Horne Island. That is if we get to take the boat ride at all—the weather doesn't seem to be cooperating.

Father Weston enters through a door on the side of the room. He greets the crowd from the pulpit and begins the service with a reading from the Book of Common Prayer. PJ waves from her pew closer to the front when she sees me. Tony isn't there because he's getting everything ready for the burial over on Horne, so she'd come and brought their daughter, Jennifer. Ms. Wilma sits in the pew in front of them—she and her son Roy have worked for the Leighs since before anyone around today can remember. I knew Roy wouldn't be here because of all his recent trouble, but I'm sure Wilma's pew feels empty without him. Cameron and Christopher, the Leigh's children, flew into town with their families yesterday, and they are sitting in the front of the church. Cameron and her husband Don live in California; Christopher and his wife Marsha live in New York, where the Leigh's are from originally. In the pew behind them, I recognize the back of one of Mrs. Leigh's two children from a previous marriage, Ann. Ann, the eldest of the two sisters, is an odd bird. She and her sister, Zada, who I realize is missing, prefer city life to Riverside Village, but that's all they seem to have in common. Ann is like a recluse, while Zada is the social butterfly. They've both been spending more time than usual in Riverside Village lately, which is part of the problem, if you ask me. A few of the Leighs' friends from church and the historical society are settled into pews. Everyone has their opinions about what's happened on Horne Island, and so seeing who came and who didn't seems to reveal something about the past.

Father Weston's voice booms through the spacious church, almost drowning the creak of the door opening behind us. I look over my shoulder and see Zada, Ann's sister, hurrying down the aisle with her friend Steven on her arm. I watch them as they hurry along the side of the pews and sit next to a dark-haired man I realize is the attorney they hired to sue their brother and sister over Horne Island. All that's settled now, but seeing him makes the somber event feel even more so. The truth is, many people in town didn't want to face Zada and Ann after the lawsuit and I think that's why the pews were so empty.

Father Weston talks about the closing of Mrs. Leigh's life, comparing her life—as well as anyone who doesn't know another person can talk about them, I suppose—to the closing of a book. Of course he didn't know Mrs. Leigh like I did, like most of the people in his church this morning. Mrs. Leigh exuded casual elegance. She always dressed in classic navy blue pants and collared dress shirts. She loved a beautiful scarf. She had quite a collection of silk scarves in different colors and patterns. Everything she owned was high quality and well made. And everything matched when she put it on—the shoes, the pants, the shirt, and the scarf. She wasn't decked out in earrings, makeup, and all that kind of stuff. She was plain. But she was elegant. And we kept her elegant. Her hair was always smoothed into place and still naturally blonde. We put lemon juice on it every week, but it never changed color or turned gray. It was her mind that didn't hold up. I suppose I'm almost grateful for that. Mr. Leigh's tragic end would have been too much even for a strong woman like her. Not knowing what happened to him makes Mrs. Leigh's death feel like another sad twist in an ongoing tragedy instead of the closing of a book.

Just as Father Weston steps away from the pulpit, someone up closer to the front of the church starts coughing and can't seem to stop. Then Cameron stands and speaks about her mother's elegance and grace, her love of horses, and how much she loved her time in Riverside Village. All this is true, but as Cameron delivers the impersonal eulogy, I think about how it may seem like those grieving the loss of someone who'd suffered with such a terrible thing as Alzheimer's for so many years would feel a sense of relief. They might share favorite stories and relax knowing their beloved didn't have to suffer any longer. With so many unanswered questions that relief isn't possible.

But maybe I'm getting ahead of myself. I shouldn't tell you about her funeral without telling you the story of the unfortunate events that have recently transpired on Horne Island. Mrs. Leigh's passing brings a dark cloud, but with the year we've had on that island, hers is only one dark cloud in a sky full. So let me start from the beginning.

October 7, 2000

I KNEW EVERYONE AT THE MARTINS' PLACE THAT night except for a debonair-looking gentleman dressed in a necktie. "Who is Zada and Ann's friend?" I asked PJ, nodding in his direction. He was standing between the Mrs. Leigh's daughters. They spent little time in River-side Village, but they'd flown in and planned this party without telling anyone why. They never came hunting and they always seemed ready to go back to New York, even when they'd just arrived. I couldn't imagine why they'd bring a friend.

"Oh, he's some big-time real estate agent from New York. Zada's friend, I guess," PJ said, as she surveyed the wine table. "Zada introduced me when I got here, but I've already forgotten his name."

"There's been quite a few real estate agents hanging around town lately, hasn't there," I said. The man looked big-time for sure. Even in the dim light I could see the cuf-flinks shining on his Brooks Brothers shirt.

"You're telling me. Tony thinks we should talk to his aunt about selling her land when prices get a little higher."

"Where'd the girls run off to?" I asked her. My daughter, Mary, and PJ's Jennifer had known each other since birth. Now they were ten and still friends.

"They're out back. Keeping themselves busy." PJ handed me a glass of white zin—my favorite—and said, "Let's go dance."

Zada and Ann hired a dance teacher to show everyone how to shag. They'd moved all the furniture against the walls so everyone had room to stumble around. The Carolina Shag seemed a little too southern for Zada and Ann, but they even seemed to be enjoying themselves. They had Mrs. Leigh set up on a wicker chair off to the side and she was smiling as Mrs. Martin knelt at her side and spoke to her. I didn't see Mr. Leigh, but he was probably out back with Tony and Mr. Martin. Mrs. Martin and Ms. Frannie, the Leigh's cook, were arranging cheese and crackers next to the wine.

The Martins' place in the Village was their summer cottage; they lived in Virginia. It was similar to others in town with a basic open front porch, large living area with wooden floors, and a fireplace in case they came in the wintertime. People who loved Riverside Village tended to really love it. The Martins loved it so much they recently bought another house, a plantation with property on the river, outside of town. All the Leigh's friends in town—over thirty people— were crowded into the living room and flowing over onto the front porch. I scanned the room for Howard, but saw him slipping out the door, probably meeting Tony outside where no one could ask them to dance. So PJ and I assumed a partnership and found a spot on the floor.

"One and two …three and four …five and six …" the instructor called out as he exaggerated the footwork and everyone else tried to follow. He made it look much easier than my feet seemed to think it was. PJ had shagged before, so she helped me figure out the steps.

"Hey, where's Ms. Wilma tonight? She should be out here dancing," I said to PJ when I started getting the steps.

"Oh, shoot, you didn't hear? Roy's in trouble," she said, swinging away from me and spinning back.

"No I didn't hear. What happened?"

"He got stopped on 95 driving a minivan packed full of marijuana. I talked to Wilma earlier. I guess Barbara asked him to drop the van off in Columbia for her friend, and Roy says he didn't know about the drugs. But they arrested him. She's up in Beaufort trying to get him out of jail."

"You're kidding!" I knew Roy had his habits, but moving drugs would be ambitious for him.

"There were pounds of it stuffed in the panels of the van body, but Roy said he didn't put it there and had no idea he was carrying it. All Roy told his mother he knew was that he was supposed to leave the van in a parking lot on the south side of the city, and Barbara's friend—whoever he was—had purchased his bus ticket home."

I'd only met Roy's girlfriend Barbara once and only knew she was a rough-looking white woman (that's how Wilma referred to her; Wilma and Roy were black) that nobody trusted, especially not Mrs. Wilma. Roy had been in minor trouble before, but this sounded serious. "Is Roy a drug dealer?"

"I don't know. But you know he did get that cell phone."

"Lot's of people get those now," I let out a laugh even though Roy being in jail wasn't funny at all. I bit my lip to regain my composure. "We need to do something. What should we do?"

"There's nothing we can do about it tonight," PJ shrugged. "If she can bail him out, then the real problem—the expensive problem—it seems to me, will be keeping him out of jail if this goes to trial."

Martha C.

That was the thing with Roy: he went to jail from time to time, often to sober up, but never for anything serious enough to keep him there. After a lesson and two songs, PJ excused herself to find the bathroom and I went to the kitchen for a glass of water. The house was built with a pantry between the living spaces and the kitchen in case of a fire. I walked through the pantry, where tablecloths and dishtowels were neatly folded and stacked on shelves.

The kitchen was small and narrow—nothing fancy. They had a long ceramic sink with the countertop on the sides and that was all the counter space. The floors were vintage green linoleum. A basic stove and refrigerator were the only appliances and all the shelves were open so you could see the few dishes they had. The house was built as a hunting and fishing cabin, and that was all they needed. They did have large-paned windows on all the kitchen walls and, although I couldn't see it because it was already dark, a million-dollar front-row view of the river. I poured myself a glass of water at the sink and then turned to get a few cubes of ice from the freezer to cool it off. The back door was open next to the fridge and I thought I heard Howard laugh from somewhere outside.

When I turned around, Zada's friend, the real estate agent, was walking up behind me. I dropped an ice cube on the floor and backed up to the refrigerator door as he slid right up in front of me. He was a tall man; his arm reached right over top of me and rested on the top of the fridge. This man wasn't bad looking—he had sandy blonde hair and small, round glasses. But he was much too forthcoming for a married woman like me. He was so close I could see the sweat on his forehead. "Excuse me," I pressed my back on the fridge.

"I don't believe we've met," he said and his mouth curled into a grin. "And I think we need to."

I froze for a second, shocked by the presence of a stranger in my personal space. His teeth were so white and straight they looked false. The music started playing again in the living room. Just then I heard the back door open and slam shut and saw Howard come around the corner behind him. The real estate agent didn't even notice anyone had walked into the room.

"Well, I'm Martha," I said, averting the unfamiliar man's gaze. "And that's my husband, Howard, right behind you."

The real estate agent straightened up and turned around. Howard, a tall man, stood with his arms crossed over his chest. Lowe knew right then and there that he'd bit the cookie. "Well," he said, clearing his throat. "It's nice to meet you Howard and Martha. I'm Steven Lowe."

Neither Howard nor I said a word.

"Well, if you don't mind, I'll just grab a beer from the fridge and get out of your way."

I looked past him at Howard, who was just standing there with his arms folded. As Mr. Lowe scurried out of the room, Howard shook his head. "You all right?"

"Yes, I'm all right." I laughed a little.

"Something tells me I don't like Zada's friend," Howard shook his head.

I rolled my eyes and followed Howard into the living room. By this time the dancing lesson had stopped for a break. Mr. Lowe had returned to his place back at Zada's side. This time they were talking to Mr. Leigh. Even at eighty-seven, Mr. Leigh was a commanding presence in any room. He was dressed in his denim shirt, khakis, and house slippers—his Riverside Village uniform. He never even bothered to pack socks when he came south. Zada's hand rested on her mother's shoulder. When she saw me, she waved me over.

Zada and her sister presented a unified front, always traveling together and pairing up. Neither woman ever married—or worked. And now that they were in their fifties, they weren't going to start. They lived in New York City and traveled to Europe, shopping and dining on their parents' money. Zada was the politician of the duo, always feigning interest where she didn't have any. I wondered what she could be up to, bringing her real estate agent friend to town. Then I saw her steal a glance at Lowe and wondered if there might be a romantic connection between the two. Ann wouldn't like that, for sure—she and Zada did everything together. Neither one of them had ever brought a boyfriend around, which wasn't so strange for Ann. But Zada was beautiful and I always thought she'd eventually find someone. We used to joke that Ann would never let Zada get married. If she was dating Lowe, it must not be exclusive, judging by the man's behavior in the kitchen.

"Martha," Zada smiled. Her eyes were lined and her cheeks were rouged. "So good to see you made it."

"Yes, Zada, well, we wouldn't miss it."

"I want you to meet my friend, Martha and Howard, this is Steven Lowe. Steven, this is Howard and Martha Smith."

Lowe nodded and reached his hand out to Howard, who didn't take it. "I believe we've already met," Howard said.

"Oh, well," said Zada, skipping over the awkwardness, "I was just telling dad that Steven wants to go hunting while we're here. I said you should all get together and go out on Horne Island."

"I'd love to see it," Mr. Lowe said. "Zada and Ann have told me all about your adventures out there."

"Well, I suppose that's up to Mr. Leigh," Howard said, crossing his arms again and standing tall.

"That's fine." Mr. Leigh's voice shook a little with age, but still boomed. "As long as Mr. Lowe here knows how to have fun. But he may have to borrow a pair of shoes." He glanced down at Lowe's polished, high-end loafers. People in Riverside Village tend to wear flip-flops and boat shoes.

Howard and I laughed. Zada shifted her weight and shook her head. "Now, Dad. I'm serious. Steven wants to experience everything Riverside Village has to offer before we go back to the city. And I think you two would have a lot to talk about."

"What makes you say that?"

Zada laughed nervously and didn't answer. Mr. Leigh was used to entertaining guests on Horne Island, and never said no to a hunting trip, but Zada and Ann weren't exactly the sporting type.

"I think it's time to get your mother back across the river," Mr. Leigh said. "Howard, would you mind helping me get Mrs. Leigh to the car."

Zada looked frustrated that her stepfather wasn't more interested in her friend.

"Now, Dad, isn't this a good reason why it might be time to move off that silly island?" Ann threw the question in. Knowing her, she'd probably been waiting all night for the opportunity to bring it up. "Think of how easy it would be to go across the street or down the road. Much easier than loading mother into a boat and ferrying her across a river."

Ann was only a year Zada's senior, but she carried herself as if she was much older. She was a homely woman. She tried to be pretty and dressed well, always wore designer clothing and nice things, but she never had the style and flair to pull it off. Every time they came to town they seemed to have something negative to say about their parents' living arrangements on Horne Island. I didn't realize at the time that there was more to their concern than the logistics of a boat ride.

Howard and I helped the Leighs to their car and stayed for another drink after they left. Later that night, when Howard and I were back at home, he asked me if I'd heard about Roy.

"I did. PJ told me. I hope Wilma's okay." I sat my purse on the kitchen counter and leaned against the cabinets.

"I talked to Tony about it. We have to wait and see what happens before we know what we can do." Marty filled a glass of water at the sink.

"You're right."

"So what do you suppose Zada has going on with that Lowe?"

"It's hard to say. But you should have seen the look on his face when I told him you were standing behind him."

Howard laughed. "I'll have to keep my eye on him." He finished his water in two gulps and placed his glass in the sink.

November 13, 2000

---⚬⚬⚬---

THE LEIGH'S HORNE ISLAND HOUSE OVERLOOKED THE creek from a high bank. I'd caught a ride with Doug that morning after he dropped the kids off to catch the school bus. Riding with Doug always put me on edge a little because his vision was so poor. His glasses were as thick as bottles. But he meant well, and as he maneuvered the boat up to the main dock, I distracted myself by admiring the way the white ranch spread across the bluff. The house wasn't palatial or extreme, but it was beautiful and large in an understated way and attention had been paid to the details of the design. I stepped off the boat and made my way up the long dock. I climbed the stairs to the front of the house, where ornate iron columns framed the porch and front door. I went around the side to the back of the house, where there was a service yard, barn, and stable, where Mr. Leigh kept his collection of horses, his prized pair of Belgian mules, and a zebra. The Leighs loved animals and even kept peacocks in their garden. Wilma and Roy's, Frannie's, and Toot's cottages stood next to the barn, and PJ and Tony lived in the house on the other side of the cabins. Just past their house was the gravel drive that led to Doug and Sue's house. Everyone must have been working or inside because I didn't see a soul.

Martha C.

I walked to the back of the Leigh's house and entered through the boiler room. The house was built in the 1960s and it was a spacious house, but not fancy. Because the people who made Crosley appliances built the place, the most modern fixture they put in was a floor heating system. The whole house was built on a cement slab wired with tubes that warmed it from the ground up in winter. This ambient warmth met me inside. I walked past the supply room and into the hall, past the pantry and into the kitchen. Inside the kitchen, wide windows lined the east-facing wall and we could see the courtyard where the Leigh's guests come and go from the front door and the main part of the house. Ms. Frannie was pulling cornbread out of the oven when I walked in.

"Good morning, Martha." Frannie looked like a cook. She was a big black woman with graying hair, dressed as always in her gray uniform and apron. She'd been working for the Leighs for years.

"It looks like I'm just in time."

"Well, we were expecting you. Coffee's ready too. Mrs. Wilma should be bringing Mrs. Leigh in any minute."

"I've brought you the paper," I said. I hung my purse and bag on the back of a chair and poured myself a cup of coffee. The Leigh's kitchen hadn't been updated since the place was built. Frannie baked her buttermilk cornbread to perfection in a thirty-year-old oven. All the appliances were old; but they worked. The sink was cast iron and the floor checkerboard linoleum. They had one of those old metal tables with the Formica top. Everything was plain and aging, even though the Leigh's had enough money for anything they wanted.

The house did have plenty of room. The kitchen connected to the main house through a butler's pantry, where all the kitchen linens, dishes, and glassware were stored. The part of the house where the Leighs actually lived had a big living room and dining room. Their bedroom and dressing rooms sat on one side of the living areas and ten bedrooms and ten bathrooms (one for each bedroom) sat on the other side. At the end of the wide hall was a large room where everyone stored their hunting gear and hung their boots to dry. And the Leighs enjoyed the house. At any given time, at least two or three of those guest rooms were occupied with some old friend or colleague of Mr. and Mrs. Leigh. They loved Horne Island and loved sharing it just as much.

"What's the word on the other side of the river?" Frannie asked as she opened her newspaper. "How's your mother?"

"Oh, she's fine. Everyone's talking about Sun City breaking ground and you know how mother likes to keep an eye on things."

"She does like to do that," Frannie scanned the headlines through her bifocals. "And look here," she said, "some developer bought Palmetto Bluff."

"I read that too," I said. "Can you imagine tearing down those woods for a golf course?"

"Is that what they're going to do?" Frannie's dark eyes widened.

"Oh, who knows? Isn't that what they always do?"

"I do know one thing," said Frannie, "Lots of the woods and trees we see today won't be here for much longer."

"And look who's here," Frannie's attention turned to Mrs. Wilma, who was wheeling Mrs. Leigh in through the butler's pantry.

"Hello, Mrs. Leigh," I said. Mrs. Leigh's face brightened. She always loved company and being where the action was, though no one could say for sure if she always recognized her company or not. I spoke to her just like she could talk to me, the same way I'd talked to her all those years. We had a wonderful connection and I knew I was always welcome at their house. I remember when they first noticed her symptoms they were driving back up to New York in Mr. Leigh's old wood-paneled station wagon. They'd barely made it north of Charleston when Mrs. Leigh became so disoriented and upset that Mr. Leigh had to stop driving and call Roy to come help him get her back to Riverside Village. From there, she went in and out for years, gradually descending into the shell of herself. The decline had been slow, but she'd arrived.

"Mrs. Leigh is all ready for you, Martha," Wilma said. "It's nice to see you. And I see you've brought me my chocolate bar," she nodded at the counter where I'd left her Hersey bar. Mrs. Wilma was in her seventies. She was shorter than me and had a long, dark face with a long chin. She wore her hair short and close-cropped, which made her face look even longer. Living on Horne Island, she couldn't just run out to the store, so I always brought her chocolate when I came. There's a lot you look forward to when you live on an island. And Mrs. Wilma loved a Hersey candy bar.

"I didn't forget about you, Ms. Wilma," I said.

"Oh, I thank you," she said, peeling open the wrapper and pulling up a seat at the table.

I started working on Mrs. Leigh while Frannie and Wilma chatted about the headlines. Mrs. Leigh was happy to be in the kitchen with the rest of us. She had the hair dryer set up in here for a reason; she didn't want to be pushed out into another room. And she didn't want me working on her in her bedroom. She wanted everybody around.

"Did you hear the good news?" Wilma asked.

"About Roy getting out of trouble?"

"Yes, ma'am. They not pressing charges."

"Oh, Ms. Wilma, I know you're relieved, but it's a shame he got in trouble in the first place. And I'm sure the lawyer fees were expensive." Roy was a live-for-today person, not a save-for-tomorrow person, so his mother had paid. I knew she mustn't have had much to start with. All the expenses associated with getting out of trouble could easily have used everything she had.

"It's just money, and so spending it on that was easy. As his mother, I could do that. What I wished I could do was prevent him from seeing that Barbara ever again."

"I sure wish he'd get whatever he has going on with that woman out of his system," I said.

"You're telling me." Mrs. Wilma shook her head. "I told him no woman he meets out at that dive in Hardeeville is going to be respectable, but you can't tell him anything. It's bad enough she white—that there is enough to make an old black lady like me nervous. And my son may not always do right. But Roy is not a drug trafficker."

"I know it," I said, not because she'd already told me, which she had, but because I wanted her to get it all out. Having a son like Roy couldn't be easy even for a strong woman like Wilma. But even more worrisome was the way Barbara seemed to have a hold on Roy. She told him where to be and when, and Roy never stood up to her. He just did what she said. Mrs. Wilma was convinced Barbara knew more about the marijuana in the car than she was saying and she believed Barbara's nefarious activities were the reason her son ended up arrested and mired in legal trouble. Barbara denied knowing anything about the marijuana too.

But no one could produce her friend who'd asked the favor in the first place. He seemed to have disappeared as soon as Roy got caught.

"Martha, my son has told me many times, looked me in the eye and everything, that he didn't know about the drugs. I prayed and prayed about it, and I believe him."

"Well, I'm grateful it's over," I said.

Mrs. Leigh rested her neck on a rolled white towel I'd used to cover the counter. Her head lay in my palm as I wet her hair with the sprayer. She closed her eyes when I started washing and she didn't open them again until I propped her back up and wheeled her to the hooded dryer. Mrs. Leigh loved getting her hair done so much that they'd brought the dryer over on the barge so she could get the salon experience without leaving the island. Wherever she was in her mind, I don't think she was ever in a place where one of my visits wasn't welcomed. But the Leighs treated everyone equally, regardless of economic or social status. They didn't treat their workers like workers. I could go over to Horne Island any time and go in the house and just sit down and talk to them. You didn't have to stay outside or in the kitchen or follow any other formalities like in some old-money families. The Leighs were wealthy and prominent, with friends like the Belmonts and Vanderbilts, but they never acted like they were better than anyone else. I'd never met anyone like them, and that made Horne Island even more special and important, especially to Wilma.

Mrs. Wilma's father worked for Mr. Leigh's father on Hilton Head Island. When they bought Horne Island in 1976, Roy was still in high school. When he finished, Mr. Leigh gave him a job. He and his mother had lived on Horne Island in the same cottage ever since. The Chesters were like family, and Mr. Leigh always helped Roy and made allowances for his habits. Roy had stability in the Leighs that most other employers would never offer. But since he'd taken up with his girlfriend, Barbara, Roy's troubles seemed to be growing. I watched Mrs. Wilma as she folded the foil and paper around the unfinished half of her candy. Her mood was lighter now that Roy was out of trouble, but the weight of her worries seemed to have aged her a decade in a year.

Frannie made it through the headlines and was reading the horoscopes in the paper aloud for us. Ms. Wilma laughed when Frannie said her professional life would take an unexpected turn. "My professional life hasn't taken an unexpected turn in decades," she shook her head.

"It say it right here in the paper, Ms. Wilma. You got to believe it," Frannie laughed. They got such a kick out of the paper. I sometimes forgot just how isolated they were on the island even though town was right across the river. Getting the newspaper before evening was a big deal for Frannie and Wilma.

I checked Mrs. Leigh's hair under the dryer and it wasn't quite ready. While she sat there I started working on her feet. I slipped them out of her shoes and rolled her pants up to her knees. When I stood up to find the skin cream I noticed Ann and Zada marching side by side through the courtyard toward the front door. Zada's scarf billowed behind her like a cape and Ann had her hands shoved in her pockets. Bursts of steam billowed from their breath meeting the chilly air.

"I see Ann and Zada are still in town," I said to Wilma.

"They sure are," she said with her eyes wide. She looked at me and then at Mrs. Leigh who was staring out from under the hood dryer. "They've been spending lots of time in Riverside Village lately. Two trips this month. Them and their friend Mr. Lowe."

"Is he Zada's boyfriend or something?"

"He too young for Ms. Zada," Wilma dismissed the idea. "Why would he be interested in her? Oh, and here they come now." Seeing the sisters through the window, she jumped up from the table and said, "I hate to leave before things get interesting, but I need to check the laundry."

"Now you can't just run off every time they come around," Frannie laughed. She had finished with the paper by this time and was making her shopping list from the store ads. Wilma was already out the back door. Leaving didn't sound like such a bad idea, but I still had Mrs. Leigh's hair to fix. I put her shoes back on her feet, straightened her pant legs, and then lifted the hood off her head. She smiled when her daughters walked in through the butler's pantry.

"Mother, I should have known we'd find you getting your hair done," Zada said as she floated across the room to her mother's side. They'd shed their coats, but you could still feel the cold coming off their skin. Ann eyed me from behind her sister. Neither one of them acknowledged Frannie or me beyond that.

"I've got fresh cornbread here, if you ladies are hungry," Frannie said. When she spoke, Zada acted almost like she hadn't seen us in the room.

"Oh, Frannie, it's kind of you to offer, but we aren't here to socialize," Zada said. Her tone hardened when she looked at me and said, "We just want to talk to Martha here about the time she's spending coming back and forth across the river to take care of mother."

"You know I don't mind doing it," I said, not sure what she was getting at.

"Of course not, but Ann and I were just talking about all the extra expenses with Mother's care, and it seems to us that the cost must double or even triple when you add on a boat ride."

Both sisters were looking at me now. Frannie's ads no longer had her attention; she was looking at the sisters.

"So how much extra do they have to pay you to come all the way over here, Martha?" Ann spoke for the first time.

With everyone's eyes on me, I felt my face get hot. I wasn't sure what I was supposed to say. What was she suggesting? "Well, they pay me a little more for the travel time. But getting Mrs. Leigh back and forth to my shop would be even more difficult."

"That's precisely what I plan on telling Dad," Zada said. "It's not easy to get mother back and forth off this island at all."

"Where is Dad?" Ann asked no one in particular.

"I believe he's out in the horse barn this morning," Frannie answered without meeting either sister's eyes.

"Thank you for your help," Zada said as she floated back out of the room with Ann following behind her.

After they'd left back through the butler's pantry and into the house, I said to Frannie, "What do you suppose that was all about?"

"Oh, it's hard to say what those two are thinking up. But it sounds to me like they don't want to pay extra to have Mrs. Leigh's help brought across the river."

"They just don't understand that's how we do things here. This isn't New York, where you can walk downstairs and have a man open the door for you and hail you a cab from the sea of them. I'd rather commute on a boat."

"Mmhmm," Wilma said. "Me too."

"Speaking of a boat ride, I need to make sure Tony doesn't leave without me." I finished up with Mrs. Leigh, said my good-byes, and went outside to find Tony. He had a meeting on the mainland at noon, so I caught a ride across the river with him. The sun had warmed up for the afternoon and the sky was blue and clear. I was grateful that the ride with Tony didn't require small talk. The ride was a pleasant twenty minutes out the creek and across the river to Riverside Village, but it was a trip I'd taken countless times since I was a kid. I could see how Ann and Zada saw it as problematic, but Wilma was right—they just didn't understand life outside the city. They'd fussed to their parents about the island before, argued about selling the place, and how silly they thought it was to spend so much time hunting birds. The Leigh's weren't young anymore, but I knew Mr. Leigh would rather die than see Horne Island developed. They may not care about updating the kitchen in the house, but they cared about that place and the people it supported, and I had a feeling Mr. Leigh would pay whatever it cost to hold on as long as he could.

November 27, 2000

THE SUN WAS SHINING ON MY PATCH OF THE DIRT ROAD, and thank goodness, because when that wind whipped up like it had been doing all afternoon I could feel it through my field jacket. Thanksgiving came and went and now winter was here. The sweet gums fiery red leaves were turning brown and it had rained almost every day that week. Catching what was left of the sunshine, I was only half-looking for deer by that time. We'd been on Indigo—the Leigh's other island, the one right next to Horne—hunting deer since late afternoon. Howard, Roy, Tony, PJ, and our friends Rooster and John were out here with me. Tony and Roy were flushing the deer in this direction from the south, and the rest of us were spaced out in stands along the road with our shotguns ready to shoot them as they came through the woods.

I climbed down from my stand to stretch my legs and walked the fifty feet or so back to the road. I hadn't seen or heard anyone shoot in at least thirty minutes. I looked down the road in both directions but still didn't see anyone. Most of the weeds along the road had started to die back. The forest spread out on both sides of me. I couldn't see it, but I wasn't far from the river.

I started scraping my boot around in the shallow ditch,

just trying to move around and keep warm more than anything else. Wet, brown leaves and acorns covered the ground. Then I kicked a hole in the leaves and something hard came up out of the pile—a bottle. Someone had probably thrown it out his truck window years before. Wet and rotting leaves covered the piece of litter, but something about the shape of it made me want to pick it up.

Mud caked the clear glass. It was a liquor bottle, flask shaped. Then I pushed a clump of leaves off the center and saw the raised palmetto design. I had unearthed a South Carolina dispensary bottle that was probably a hundred years old. These were used when Governor Tillman took over state liquor sales in the late 1800s. I'd seen them around and heard of other people finding them, but I'd never found one myself. I wiped the face of it on the side of my pants and revealed the palm-tree design. Feeling luckier than if I'd shot a deer, I stuffed the bottle inside the deep interior pocket of my coat where no one would see it and then zipped my coat up all the way. I'd have to wait and tell Howard about it after we got home. Mr. Leigh wouldn't have cared that I'd kept it, but someone else might try to get it from me so they could keep it.

The excitement sustained me until the sun fell a little more and the cold started biting. A sparse fog had penetrated the woods behind me, giving the Spanish moss-draped trees an eerie look. The forest was silent except for a few birds. I could hear myself swallow until a gunshot echoed from down the road. I held my breath for a moment to listen harder. It came from Howard and PJ's direction. Then another shot fired from somewhere in the opposite direction. That had to have been Rooster—he took the furthest post past mine. At least someone had seen something to shoot at, I thought, even though I'd been so preoccupied that I'd almost forgot to watch for the deer to come through. Now I was ready to get back. We never hunted past sunset, and I didn't like riding across the river in the dark. The darkness could be so complete that I couldn't tell which way I was coming and which way I was going. It was the strangest feeling. The fog, if it thickened, would only make it worse.

I heard Howard's whistle coming from down the road before I saw him. When we were out, he always whistled as he approached me so I'd know it was him and not something I should be aiming at. He looked like a shadow in the coming darkness until the fog spit him out and I could see him right in front of me.

"Did you get anything?" he was smiling because he already knew the answer.

"No, sir, I didn't. At least not any deer."

"Well, we better head back before it gets too dark." We walked down the muddy road, side-by-side, toward the dock.

"I told you we could stay out later if everyone else wanted to."

"Yeah, but I've got to live with you when we get home. And we got plenty of deer already."

Back at the dock, the fog blanketed the water. The house, which sat only three hundred yards or so from the water, was hidden. Although considerably smaller and simpler than the Horne Island house, the Indigo house was nice enough. Inside it had a big, open room with a kitchen in the back and bar seating at a counter in the middle. And then there were two screened-in breezeways, one on either side, which led to a bedroom and bathroom. When Cameron and her family came, they loved staying on Indigo. The problem I had with the Indigo house was that the Leighs didn't use it often, and everyone passing by along the river seemed to know it, so they got a lot of squatters. We were always finding garbage and other signs that people had come off the river and spent time in the house.

"Roy, Tony, and Rooster killed their deer early in the day, so they've been drinking to keep warm," Howard said. "And I believe PJ went inside to change. Her feet and legs were pretty muddy."

"I'll go in and find her," I said, parting ways with Howard and walking toward the house. I saw PJ's muddy boots outside the door, then it swung open and there was PJ, warm and dry in jeans and tennis shoes.

"Hey," she said.

"Hey. Did you shoot anything?"

"No, but I fell in the mud," she laughed. "Do you need in the house?"

"No, I was just coming to find you. The boys are all down at the dock."

"Well, we better get over there before they drink all the beer." She and I crossed the yard, but then she stopped. "I forgot my boots outside the door. You go ahead, I'll run back and get them." She jogged away from me and I kept walking toward Tony, Roy, Howard, Rooster, and John. They were standing in a circle by the dock, beers in hand, talking and laughing about something.

"She doesn't compare to that girl you were with the other night, Tony," Roy was laughing as I walked up.

"She's all right," Tony said. They hadn't seen me.

"Who are you talking about?" I said. The five of them looked at me like I'd caught them with their hands in the cookie jar. Howard shook his head and the rest of them busted out laughing.

"What's so funny?" PJ said, walking up behind me, slightly winded from her jog.

"Oh, Tony was just telling us about that time he and Howard rode the horses into the hotel on Hilton Head." Roy covered for them without skipping a beat.

"That was funny as hell," Rooster said guiltily.

"We better get going," Howard said.

Tony, PJ, and Roy were taking two of the six deer with them back to Horne Island; the rest of us were taking the other four deer back across the river where Rooster was going to butcher them. Roy had already trucked the deer out of the woods and had them piled at the end of the dock. The tide had fallen all the way, leaving the ramps at a full pitch down to the water. Indigo had two docks—a service dock and a main dock near the house. We were at the main dock, which jutted out thirty yards or so from the shore and then had a metal ramp that tipped down to a lower level floating on the water where the two boats were tied.

"Are four people and four deer going to fit in our boat?" I asked Howard. We were in a fourteen-foot boat that hardly fit four bodies, let alone eight.

"We'll be all right," he said. "Let's just get everything down there and we'll figure it out."

This dock didn't get as much traffic as the service one and bird droppings and algae covered the metal. With the wet weather and the steep pitch, we all stood at the top wondering how to get down. After standing there, thinking about it for a minute, I said, "Well, I guess I'll go first."

I sat down on my behind, being careful with the bottle in my coat pocket and holding onto the grips so I wouldn't slip off into the water, and slid. Once I started going, I found out soon enough, there was no way to stop. The ramp was so slippery that I slid, hitting each cleat like a speed bump—*bump, bump, bump*—all the way down to the bottom. When I landed, everyone was watching me wide-eyed from the top of the dock.

"Are you all right?" PJ yelled.

"Ugh, yes, I'm fine." My rear was cold and wet, but I was thrilled I didn't fall in. "Y'all can go ahead and laugh now."

And they did, all six of them laughed until they slid down the dock too. It was so steep and slippery, sliding turned out to be the only way down. We slid the deer, coolers, guns, and everything else down the ramp. Howard and Roy loaded the deer into the boats. They landed on the floor like sacks of grain, each weighing at least eighty or ninety pounds, between the bench seats. I stepped aboard and took the seat at the bow of the boat, then Rooster and John each boarded and sat in the middle, sinking the boat down low in the water. When Howard stepped in and took his seat in the back, only inches of hull prevented the river from spilling over and swamping us.

"Whatever you do," John said as Howard started the engine, "don't rock the boat."

"No kidding," Rooster laughed. "Y'all know I can't swim, right? Don't rock the boat."

I heard Howard chuckling behind them. John and Rooster had a glassy-eyed look that suggested they'd been in and out of the beer cooler all afternoon.

Howard eased the boat away from the dock after we said our goodbyes to PJ, Tony, and Roy. The black water was smooth as glass and the fog obscured the marsh on either side of us. With the boat so loaded down, we couldn't go fast, and the engine grumbled through the dark. Although we could barely see them, we followed the other boat through the creek until they turned to head toward the dock on Horne and we continued down the creek toward the Chrystal River.

We'd only been on the water for five minutes when John said he needed a cigarette. As soon as he moved his arm and shifted his weight, the boat tipped to the side and water spilled over the gunwale.

"Shit, what are you doing?" Rooster yelled. It wasn't much water, but it was enough to worry him.

"I'm just trying to get a smoke," John laughed.

"We're taking on water," Rooster said with drunken affront. "Sit still."

John couldn't get his cigarette lit in the wind and asked Rooster to help him block. As soon as Rooster shifted his weight to cover John, the boat tipped again, in the opposite direction.

"If y'all keep wiggling around, the boat will sink," Howard said, laughing at them both. "Either that or you'll burn the boat right out from under us with your cigarette and we'll all be swimming home."

"Oh, no. I told you I can't swim," Rooster said. Rooster would go across the water, but he didn't like to be in it. "But while you've got your cigarettes out, John, mind giving me one?"

John passed him the cigarettes and a lighter. The engine groaned as it pushed us toward the mouth of the creek. We were only going about five miles an hour. I couldn't see anything through the dark and fog. The beam of the boat's spotlight cast a pale glow on the marsh grass. The wind chilled me through my coat. We were close to the mouth of the river, though I couldn't tell exactly where. That's when I heard what sounded like a woman's voice. "Did y'all hear that?"

"I thought I heard someone yelling," said Rooster, exhaling a dense cloud of smoke.

Howard cut the motor and we all listened to the water lapping, the wind rustling the grass, and then the sound of a conversation coming from somewhere up ahead. Howard shined the spotlight in the direction of the sound. Nothing but fog. He started the motor again and ran it even slower than we'd been going. As we went, he swept the beam back and forth across the span of the creek. The light glittered in the fog. That's when I saw the boat.

The white whaler emerged from the fog and shadows. They were stopped near the mouth of the river and the tone in the voices suggested they were in distress. As Howard pulled our boat in closer, he called out to them.

"Yes," a man's voice called back. "We broke down and need help."

The voice sounded northern, but the fog obscured the faces until we got right up beside them—it was Zada and her friend, Lowe. Howard and John reached out to grab the side of their boat.

"What in the world are you two doing out here in the dark?" I asked her.

"Oh, Martha, Howard, it's you," Zada said with nervous relief. She had a towel wrapped around her shoulders and disheveled look that I'd never seen on her before. "We broke down, there's something wrong with the boat."

"Well, you're lucky; we were just coming from Indigo," Howard said. "How long have you been here?"

"Long enough to nearly freeze to death," she said.

"What seems to be the problem?"

"Well, the engine just quit," Lowe chimed in. "I have to admit I'm not familiar with boat engines."

"Can you give us a tow?" Zada asked. "We're headed to Indigo."

"I'm not sure we can," Howard said. "We're overloaded at the moment. But if I can't get you going, I'll come back for you. What happened when it quit?"

"It just sputtered out and died," Lowe said.

"Almost sounds like you're out of gas," Rooster said.

"It does, doesn't it," Howard said. "Did you check your tank?"

"Well, no, I guess I didn't," Lowe shook his head and ran his fingers through his hair. He looked just as rattled and out of place on the river as Zada. "I'm not sure I even know how to do that."

Rooster and John looked at each other and snickered. Even I knew how to check the gas on a boat.

"Down under the engine there should be two orange gas tanks," Howard said. "If you pull them out from under there, you'll be able to tell if there's anything in them."

Lowe moved to the back of the boat. They sat higher on the water, so we couldn't see what he was doing, but I heard him shuffling around. Then he said, "Well, it seems like one is empty and the other is full. What do you suppose that means?"

"It means you need to switch the gas line from one tank to the other," Howard said.

Rooster couldn't hold it in anymore—he busted up laughing. John was laughing too.

"Okay," Lowe said, coming back into view. "How do I do that?"

"You just unhook the tube from one and hook it on the other," Howard said. "I'd have to see it to explain it any better than that." I couldn't tell if he was getting angry or just trying to hold back his own laughter.

Lowe disappeared again toward the back of their boat. It sounded like he was moving boxes. Then Zada said, "Not like that, Steve, you're doing it wrong."

"What do you mean I'm doing it wrong?" he said back to her, defending himself.

"Don't do that or you're going to break it!"

And he yelled back, "Damn it, Zada, this was your idea coming out here in the dark, being secretive about it. Now you're mad at me?"

"Is everything okay up there?" I yelled, realizing we were witnessing something between these two that they maybe hadn't wanted anyone to see.

My call was met with silence. Then after a few seconds Zada said, "Yes, we're fine. Howard, do you think you can come up here and change out the tanks?"

Howard rolled his eyes and said, "Yes, ma'am, I'll come aboard. Lowe, you should come over here and steady the boat while I climb up."

With Rooster hanging on from our side and Lowe hanging on from theirs, Howard rose from his seat and, putting all his weight on their boat to avoid swamping ours, pulled himself up and over the gunwale.

"It looks like you guys were having a good time on Indigo today," Lowe said to Howard once he was aboard. "Did you hunt those deer?"

"We did."

"I always wanted to try hunting," Lowe said. "Seems like it would be nice to spend the day out in the woods."

"Well, I hope you're better at hunting than boating, or you'd be in trouble," I heard Howard mutter under his breath. Howard leaned over out of view and I heard him shuffling something. "Looks like we're not the only ones carrying a load this evening. What is all this stuff?"

"Well," Zada said after a pause, "My friend Steve has decided to stay in Riverside Village for a while and we're getting him set up at the Indigo house."

"It looks like you're going into business over there, Steve," Howard said. "You've got a new computer and a fax machine. This must be a working vacation."

"I suppose you could call it that," Lowe said.

"Just don't worry about that," Zada said quickly. "I want to get off this boat."

I didn't know Zada well, but I did know what it looked like when someone got caught. They sounded like they were up to something. I sat there hoping Howard would keep pressing them, but he just switched the tank, pumped the bulb, and told Lowe to try starting it again. A moment later their engine sputtered to life and Howard was sitting on the edge of their boat ready to climb back down to ours. When he did, the boat dipped deeper in to the creek but didn't take on any more water. I could see Rooster holding his breath and gripping his seat.

"Oh, thank you so much," Zada said. "We could have been out here all night."

"What do you suppose that was all about?" Howard asked me as their boat continued down the creek and disappeared in the fog.

"Hard to say," I said. "But it sure looked like a lover's quarrel was going on when we pulled up."

"I believe you're right about that," Howard said.

"He's such a creep," I said. "He's probably only after her for her money."

"I don't know, but you should have seen everything they had in the boat—a computer and a printer, all brand-new."

"You know," Rooster said, "if that fella thinks he's going to be spending time on Indigo, he better learn how to switch the gas tank on a boat, or he ain't ever gonna leave Indigo."

"You think he can swim, Rooster?" John teased.

"Man, that ain't nice." He shook his head and laughed. "I'll tell you what, though, I wouldn't want to stay on Indigo by myself. Too many unexpected visitors wandering up at night."

Howard started our motor back up and steered us out toward the river, and I rode the rest of the way home thinking about Lowe and Zada and what they might be up to. I couldn't help feeling like something underhanded was starting to take shape in the fog.

December 11, 2000

‒‒‒‒‒‒ ⚬⚬⚬ ‒‒‒‒‒‒

A FEW WEEKS AFTER OUR STRANGE ENCOUNTER WITH Zada and her friend in the creek, a big party of us went dove hunting on Horne Island. It had been a beautiful afternoon. The way the sun fell on the brown fields illuminated everything with a golden glow. When we rode along the Evening Trail home, the Leighs and the Martins rode while Roy drove the wagon. The rest of us followed on horseback.

As per tradition, the Leighs and their guests were always dropped first at the front of the house while the rest of us rode around and parked and unloaded the hunting equipment in the back. But in those later years I liked to accompany Mrs. Leigh into the house, so when we all came around front, I jumped down off my horse. Without even thinking about it, I reached for Mrs. Leigh's arm and walked alongside her as we approached the front door. Then right before we got to the porch, I'll never forget it, Mrs. Martin turned and said with affront, "Now, Martha, you can't come any further than here."

People let you know their status is higher than yours in many ways, large and small. And I knew my walking in the front door went against tradition. But I'd escorted Mrs. Leigh inside her front door many times and it took me a second to realize why Mrs. Martin was upset. I just looked at her, and before I could arrive at a response, Mr. Leigh swooped in and hooked my arm in his.

"Come on, Caroline, let's go inside," he said with a glance at Mrs. Martin. He always called me Caroline, and he always treated me and everyone else like a friend, not someone of a lower class, even though he was the man who signed everyone's checks. We were all part of the hunting party to Mr. Leigh, and Mrs. Martin certainly didn't argue with him.

After getting Mrs. Leigh inside, Mr. Leigh and I walked out through the back. I was looking for Howard and he needed to talk to Tony. Mr. Leigh was very strong, still in good shape, and, oh, he was a brilliant man. I wish everyone could have known him. He treated me as an equal, but I held him in the highest regard. Lots of people did. When we walked out the door, we found Howard and Tony talking near the barn and walked across the yard to them.

"Tony," Mr. Leigh boomed when we approached.

"Mr. Leigh, sir, it was a fine afternoon."

"It was. I believe we showed the Martins how to have a good time." Mr. Leigh beamed down at Tony. At 6'5", Mr. Leigh looked down at everyone. "But before I forget to ask you, Ann wants a Jeep on the island. Would you mind bringing one from the mainland house over on your next barge trip."

"I will see that it gets done tomorrow," Tony said. "Is Ann planning on staying for a while?"

"Who knows," Mr. Leigh shrugged. Neither Ann nor Zada liked spending time on Horne Island, but they always got what they wanted regardless of the expense. Ann could have asked for a helicopter and probably gotten it.

Just then Zada and her friend Mr. Lowe walked around the house and joined us.

"Good evening," Lowe said. "Zada was just showing me around your lovely grounds."

Zada stood next to him smiling. "What are you doing out this evening?" she said.

"Oh, we're just finishing up from an afternoon in the dove fields," Mr. Leigh said with a hint of suspicion. "What about you two?"

"Oh, you were dove hunting? I told you, Daddy, that Steven would like to go hunting with you before we have to go back to New York."

"That's right," Mr. Leigh smiled. "Are you still looking to spend an afternoon in Riverside Village's finest dove fields, Lowe? We were talking about shooting on Indigo later this week."

"Well, sir, I was hoping to see more of Horne. Could we hunt here instead?"

"I suppose it doesn't make any difference," Mr. Leigh said. "You are the guest, after all."

"Yes," Lowe said. He ran his fingers through his hair the same way he'd done so many times that night we found them stranded in the creek. "Yes, and when can we go on this hunt?"

"Well, we go hunting almost every afternoon," Leigh said. "You can come anytime. How about tomorrow?"

"Oh, that soon. Well, I guess I need some advanced notice," he stumbled on his words as if Mr. Leigh intimidated him. Mr. Leigh intimidated a lot of people. "You know, so I can make arrangements ahead of time."

"Well, what kind of arrangements do you need to make, Mr. Lowe?"

"Oh, I don't know, I just like to plan ahead, I guess."

"You just let me know when you're ready," Tony said, chuckling at the city boy.

Zada shot Tony a poison look. "How about next Friday?" she said.

"Anytime is fine with me," Mr. Leigh said. He looked at his watch and then past Zada, like he was losing interest in the conversation.

"That's fine for me too," Tony said. "Mr. Lowe, is that enough advanced notice for you to get your plans made?"

"Uhhh, that's fine." Lowe ran his hand through his hair. "That's fine, right Zada?"

"Good. Then it's all settled. Friday on Horne Island. But what part of the island? Where will you be, Tony?"

Tony and Mr. Leigh exchanged looks that suggested they had no idea why it mattered.

"Why don't you tell us?" Mr. Leigh said.

"How about that one you guys are always talking about, the one where you got all those extra doves last time we were here?" Zada said.

"Oh, you mean Seabrook Gate?" Tony said. "That's fine. Still some of our best hunting."

"Yes, Seabrook Gate, that's right. And where is that on the island, exactly?" Zada pressed.

Tony looked at her suspiciously. Mr. Leigh excused himself to rejoin his company inside.

"I'm just curious," she explained.

"It's down on the top end," Tony said.

"That's perfect," she said, nodding to Mr. Lowe.

"If you'll excuse me," Tony said. "I need to check on things with Roy."

When he stepped away, Howard and I were left with Zada and Lowe. The four of us exchanged awkward glances, then I said, "Well, Howard and I were just leaving, weren't we, Howard?"

"We were," he said.

"Have a good evening," Zada smiled, linked her arm in Mr. Lowe's, and continued on their way across the yard to the garden.

DECEMBER 15, 2000

Mother's house sat right next to the public boat launch on the mainland side of the river. The cottage was built in the 1950s after a fire burned down a hotel that used to be there. From her favorite seat on the porch, she could watch the boats come and go, see who was up to what, and take in the view of the expansive and natural river. That's where I found her on Friday morning, sitting, taking in the view.

"Just look at that Monstrosity, Martha." She pointed at a barge parked out in the middle of the river. It was so big it had a crane on it.

"Good morning, Mother. What's going on out there?"

"Didn't you hear? They're doing utility work—building that new line across." She had a blanket wrapped around her and a cup of tea steamed from her hands. "They'll be out there working on it for months, I heard."

"Well they've sure got a big boat." I watched two men in hard hats move about the barge until a stiff breeze blew in right off the water and sent a shiver through me. "Aren't you cold sitting out here?"

"Oh, it's not that bad. The tea's hot if you want some. I just poured mine."

"I'll go fix a cup," I said. "But I can't stay long." Inside Mother's house was quiet and clean. A small fire crackled in the hearth and the tea was still hot enough to feel it through my cup.

"What are you up to today?" she asked when I rejoined her.

"Oh, I'm running errands. Howard's over on Horne Island, hunting doves through the afternoon. We're having PJ and Tony for dinner this weekend and I needed to get some things done."

"Hunting doves?" she said.

"Yes, a big group of them. Even Zada's friend from out of town is going," I said, sipping my tea. The Leighs loved hunting doves. And in the southern tradition, part of their fun was throwing a big party and having company come and hunt on their property, which they employed people—Tony, Howard, and a few others—to maintain as ideal bird habitat. They spent days in spring and summer planting corn, sunflowers, brown top, millet, and other food plants to attract the birds to the fields. They had certain spots that were better than others that everyone knew about, like Home Shoot, Savannah Pond, Big Duck, Baynard, Bennett, Piney Woods, and Donkey Pasture. And they had secret good spots that only a few people knew about, like Seabrook Gate. Dove season was a big deal on Horne Island.

"I wonder if they'll run into the archeologists," Mother said thoughtfully. She gazed off at the river. The sun was supposed to come out later, but clouds had blocked it all morning.

"What do you mean, archeologists?" I asked after taking a moment to absorb her comment.

"Yes," she said. "They're digging on Horne Island today."

"Mother, what are you talking about?" I looked at her, huddling over her tea.

"The archeologists digging on Horne Island. I saw them leave for there this morning."

"Well, I didn't hear about any archeologists."

"I hadn't either until I saw them pull up to launch their boat. There were several of them, so I walked over to ask what they were doing."

"And they said they were archeologists?" The idea of archeologists being out there wasn't unbelievable, but it seemed like the kind of thing I would have heard about.

"Yes, they did," she said, meeting my stare. "You're talking to me like I'm losing my mind."

"I'm sorry. It's just strange Howard didn't mention it at all. Where did they say they were digging?"

"They didn't. I saw the boat and actually thought they'd be fishing for horseshoe crabs, which was why I went over and asked in the first place. Did you see that article in the paper?"

She was talking about an article that had just run about horseshoe crab blood being used to treat cancer, and yes, I'd seen it.

"Well, these gentleman said they were archeologists," she said.

"Huh," I said. "They could probably find all kinds of stuff over there. In fact, I just found one of those old South Carolina Dispensary bottles on Indigo the other day. Did I tell you about that?"

"I believe it," Mother said. We chatted about my errands and her plans for the weekend. I asked if she needed anything while I was out; she said no, but I poked around in her refrigerator before I left just to make sure. Mother was in excellent shape for her advanced age, but I still worried just because she was my mother.

I left her to get my shopping done without giving another thought to what she'd said about the archeologists. I didn't give it another thought all day until Howard came home that evening. I could tell he was mad about something because of the way he pulled the door closed a little too hard. I had a chicken roasting in the oven and was loading the dishwasher. When I asked him what was the matter, he dropped his coat on the dining room chair and let out a long sign before telling me what happened.

That afternoon, Howard explained, everyone was excited. The Leighs' friends had come down from New York, plus Zada and Ann were there with their Steve Lowe. Tony, knowing not everyone in the party was experienced, took them to one of the best shoots on the island: Seabrook Gate. This particular shoot got its name probably because the farmer who owned the place back in the 1800s used to have a gate there. The gate was gone, but the name stuck. Anyways, they got everyone set up around the field. They had plenty of room for everyone to have about fifty feet between himself and the next shooter. Tony and Howard explained to Lowe how not to kill anyone. Shoot only at ten o'clock or higher. If you shoot lower than that, you'll hit someone in the face. If the birds come in low, you call low bird, and nobody shoots at them. Then they all took their positions and watched for birds to shoot.

By three in the afternoon or so, the birds were flying well. Nice and high, for the most part. The sun had come out, but it didn't get too hot. Shotgun blasts filled the air and their dove vests. Mr. Leigh, Tony, and a few others filled their limits early, so they switched stands with those who weren't doing as well. But the Leighs weren't sticklers for the hunting regulations. They didn't care who hunted deer on the island or when, as long as it didn't interfere with their activities. Howard used to be out hunting deer the same time the Leighs had a party out hunting birds on a different part of the island and they'd never cross paths. They didn't worry about start times—sometimes they went out shooting in the morning, fished through midday, and then went back out shooting before dinner. And if someone shot extra birds, they'd just divvy them up amongst those who hadn't killed their limit, and sometimes they didn't even bother to do that. They owned the whole island and the one next to it and it wasn't like the game warden was snooping around watching them. At least they never thought anyone was watching.

"The birds were just flying too good. Everyone was having a good time—a picture perfect afternoon." As he removed his hat and various pieces of hunting gear, he placed it on our dining room table—Howard's closet during the season.

"So what's the matter then?" I rinsed a glass, placed it in the top rack, and then turned to face him.

"Well, after a few hours, we're all tired and wrapping up, and out of nowhere…" he paused as if he were thinking about what to say next, "six game wardens come rising up out of the woods."

"Game wardens?"

"Yes, ma'am, the DNR had been out there all afternoon, just watching us, waiting to count our birds."

"You're kidding." Then I remembered Mother's archeologists.

"I wish I was. Calvin Espy, Gentry Miller, that officer who busted Rooster on the boat that time—all of them. They'd parked their boat on the back end of the island, hiked through the woods, and surrounded the field."

"You'll never believe this, but Mother saw a DNR boat leave from the landing this morning and they told her they were archeologists working on Horne Island."

"Archeologists? Well, these weren't any archeologists. They were waiting to bust us with too many birds."

Their story about being archeologists was actually easier to believe than what Howard was telling me. In all the years we'd been hunting on that island, no game warden had ever come around to see what we were doing. The DNR never paid Horne Island any attention. Having a team of them waiting on the very day in the very field where everyone would be hunting couldn't possibly be a coincidence.

"Every single one of us got a ticket, Martha," he continued, pulling an empty chair from the table and dropping himself into it. "You should have seen Mr. Leigh—he was furious. Dumbfounded and furious. Even his friends from New York got tickets. We have to go to federal court."

"So what do you suppose made the DNR think they had something to investigate out there?"

"That's a good question. Someone must have tipped them off." Howard unlaced his boots.

"It sounds like someone did more than tip them off." I closed the dishwasher and tried to recall everything mother had said. It was too late to call her. "It sounds to me like they knew exactly where y'all would be and when."

Howard didn't talk for a moment, as if he was letting this thought roll around in his mind. He fiddled with a pair of gloves that on the table. Then he scowled. "If I didn't know any better, I'd say Zada's friend Mr. Lowe had something to do with this."

"Now, Howard, you can't prove that," I said, hoping to diffuse his anger. He seemed to have a grudge against that man since he put a move on me in the kitchen at the Martins' place.

"No, Martha, he's been hanging around, trying to buddy up to Mr. Leigh, trying to impress everyone, but at the same time he's sneaking stuff over to Indigo, he doesn't want the Leighs to know he's dating their daughter. He can't be trusted."

"Yes, but he got a ticket too, didn't he?" I opened the oven to check the chicken. "This won't be ready for another thirty minutes or so."

"He did, that's true," Howard conceded. "I can't tell what that guy is up to. He seemed like he was genuinely enjoying himself hunting today, but I just don't think he can be trusted."

"Why would he want to get everyone in trouble? He seemed so interested in hunting."

"Interested, all right. Interested in busting up the party, maybe. Whoever it was sure got everyone in trouble." Howard stood and pushed his chair in, and headed out to the garage, where he stayed until dinner.

February 16, 2001

---·ᢒᢒᢒ·---

HOWARD FOUND OUT A FEW WEEKS LATER EXACTLY
what Mr. Lowe was up to. After the holidays and the end of
dove season, the Leighs went to New York for a month. They
kept an apartment in Manhattan and also owned another
house in the Hamptons. In the meantime, Mr. Lowe spent
quite a bit of time on Indigo Island. Not even the trip to
federal court over the dove-hunting incident deterred him
from Riverside Village. PJ told me she'd encountered him
a few times on Horne Island; he seemed to be just poking
around, spending time, making friends with everyone. She
insisted it was because he wanted to marry Zada and was
probably sniffing around at what he might inherit if he did.
We could all be working for Mr. Lowe one day, she laughed.
Howard didn't think it was funny. His suspicions of Mr.
Lowe only continued to grow.

When they went to court up in Charleston, Mr. Leigh
graciously paid everyone's fines. He felt terrible that his
guests had been so inconvenienced, and he kept asking
around to find out how the DNR had become suspicious
in the first place. No one seemed to know. But all ten of
them, even the Leigh's friends from New York had to fly
in to appear, sat in the courtroom, in the defendants' seats,
for getting carried away in the dove fields. Howard, who

was still angry about the whole thing, said something about the way Mr. Lowe kept running his hands through his hair and fidgeting in his seat made him seem stranger than ever.

"The way he kept apologizing to everyone," Howard told me afterward, "it was like he was guilty of something more than shooting too many doves."

Then one morning Howard went out deer hunting on the backside of Horne. He was walking through the woods on the south side of the island, not far from the road and Seabrook Gate, when heard a Jeep out driving and come to a stop out on the road near where he stood. He couldn't see anything through the dense shrubbery. Curious about who was out there—he hadn't expected to run into anyone—he crept toward where the sound stopped. The first thing he saw, coming through the woods, was the Jeep Roy had brought over for Ann. Ann was in New York—hadn't been on the island since December, in fact, when he thought about it. Every time he'd seen the Jeep it had been parked in the barn, taking up space. So who was driving it now? Howard was dressed in full camouflage, and he used that to his advantage. He bellied down. He could hear voices, a male voice, talking to someone else. Then, peering through the brush on the edge of the woods, he caught a glimpse of a coiffed, blond head he immediately recognized as Mr. Lowe.

"Do you see what I mean, gentlemen? We need to come up with a plan for this section that will win over Leigh's favor. It has to be good," Lowe said.

"You know the landscape just begs for a golf course."

"Now we're talking," Lowe said.

Howard could hear the excitement in the man's voice. "This could be a huge money-maker for us, gentleman. But we have to win over the old man's favor. Let's take a ride out to the end of this road. I want to show you those million-dollar water views I was telling you about."

Howard sat there in the brush listening as Lowe and whoever he was talking to—two men in suits was all he could tell—talked about Horne Island like it was for sale. As the Jeep engine came to life, shifted into gear, and drove away, Howard realized exactly what Mr. Lowe had come to Riverside Village to do.

Howard couldn't get out of the woods fast enough. He didn't even stick around to shoot a deer. He went straight back to the boat and across the river and had Cameron on the phone before he changed out of his hunting clothes. Of course Cameron knew nothing about Lowe, but she did say Ann and Zada had been pestering them to sell. They were always fretting about how much money their parents spent keeping the island up, but money seemed infinite for the Leighs. Mr. Leigh's father had been a successful inventor and an investment banker. He held patents for all sorts of military equipment and other pieces of technology. But Ann and Zada, never having worked a day in their lives, must have thought their inheritance and funding for their lavish lifestyle was being wasted on a hunting retreat their parents were getting too old to enjoy. And maybe they had a point. But the Leighs owned two islands, for goodness sake. Money was no object. But I knew for sure that if Lowe was sneaking around and having developers out, then Ann and Zada must have put him up to it.

Cameron promised Howard she would stop their scheming right away. She called Lowe and told him where to stick his development plans. Then she told him to get all his stuff off Indigo and Horne, or wherever he was hiding it. And finally, she called her father. The Leighs flew back to Riverside Village that weekend. I was at the house, cutting camellias so they'd be there when Mrs. Leigh arrived, when Roy brought them over in the boat. Mr. Leigh barely said a word to anyone as he marched into the house. By this time, everyone had heard what happened. We were all shocked that Ann and Zada coordinated such a plot, but it sure explained a lot about Mr. Lowe's presence. He'd been snooping around, sizing the place up, this whole time. That man was walking around, counting the money he'd make if the deal went through.

Making matters worse, PJ called me the night before, fuming with suspicion.

"Tony told me to go to his mother's house for the weekend," she huffed. "When I asked why, he said he couldn't say. He couldn't say! What the hell is that supposed to mean?"

"Well, maybe he wants to surprise you or something."

"Ha," she laughed viciously. "I wish. You know what I think, don't you Martha."

I did, but I didn't say.

"I think he's going to have a girlfriend out for the weekend."

"Now you don't know that."

"No, I don't. But you have to admit I have reason to be suspicious."

She did have good reason. But she didn't have proof. Rumors, I told her, weren't a reason to condemn a man. And I did believe that. I said the same thing to Howard before he had proof of Lowe's plot. You can't accuse people of wrongdoing without some kind of evidence; and hearing about it isn't evidence.

When my basket was full of camellia blossoms, I went around the house to the back door and into the kitchen. Frannie was stirring a simmering pot of something on the stove, and Ms. Wilma was counting silverware, getting ready to set the table.

"Oooh, those are pretty," Ms. Wilma said when she saw the flowers. Camellias were Mrs. Leigh's favorite. She had several bushes outside in the yard she loved so much she hired a horticulturist to come all the way from Florida when they got some parasite that nearly killed every last bush. That year I went all around Riverside Village, cutting camellias from everyone's yards, so Mrs. Leigh could still have some on her table.

"Do you think these flowers will soften Mr. Leigh's mood?"

"Oh, no," Ms. Wilma laughed and gave me a knowing look. "I'm 'fraid nothin' gonna soften Mr. Leigh's mood today," she said even though she didn't have to. We all knew Ann and Zada and their friend Mr. Steven Lowe were in trouble. Zada and Ann arrived a few hours later, no doubt summoned by their stepfather.

The next day, Howard and I took the boat to Horne Island late in the afternoon. As far as we knew, Ann, Zada, and Steven Lowe were packing their outpost on Indigo. Mr. Leigh's anger must not have left enough room for the plotting stepdaughters in the Horne Island house. Ms. Wilma told me that no one had seen them since they arrived the night before. If they hadn't had their big confrontation yet, we all knew it was coming. I could feel the tension circling in the air like vultures as soon as I stepped off the boat. That, and the acrid smell of smoke. Not only had a Leigh family drama descended upon the island, but it was time for the spring burning, which was why we were there. Every year they burned the fields and forest understory to clear out the dead brush before everything started growing again. The conditions for such an activity had to be precise—it couldn't be too dry or too wet, the wind had to be blowing just so, and they couldn't risk disturbing any nesting birds. Tony had cleared it with the fire department on the mainland days before, in case anyone called to report smoke and flames, they'd know not to sound the alarm. They couldn't just burn whenever they wanted, which was why we had all gathered outside to do the job despite the trouble smoldering inside the family's house.

As frightening as starting a forest fire sounds, they used all hands available to watch it and keep it under control. I didn't help burn every year—most of the time I liked to sit and watch the fire glowing at nighttime from my porch across the river. Even from that distance, the long line of low-burning coals glowed red in the darkness. I enjoyed watching it so much, but I also enjoyed helping them burn. Everyone loved to burn—even Ms. Wilma looked forward to it. PJ had gone to Tony's mother's house in Georgia for the weekend—though no one had any idea why, at least not that they were sharing—so Howard said they could use the extra hand and I couldn't refuse. Even though burning was a safe and common practice, something about standing in a burning field felt dangerous and exhilarating.

"Y'all ready to start a fire?" Tony said to Howard and me when we walked up. He was leaning against his Jeep with his arms folded, waiting to drive us to the site. "We're working on the bottom end of the island. Roy's already set the perimeter, now we're just starting to torch."

As we rode, I resisted the urge to give him a hard time about sending my friend off without an explanation. Tony wasn't the sort of man you could question. Good-looking, he dressed always in a red hat and a western-style shirt. He was a good friend of Howard's and loyal to the Leighs and everyone else on Horne, but the way his eyes glimmered gave the impression he had something cooking that he wasn't telling you about. With him, everything was revealed on a need-to-know timeline. PJ might not know what he was up to for weeks if ever. Tony's blue eyes and confident swagger were difficult to resist, and the way he always seemed to attract attention from women, she had good reason to suspect he was running around on her. No one ever really knew what Tony was thinking, and he liked it that way.

The smoke thickened as we approached the site and filled the air in heavy plumes over the field. I could barely tell who was who under their masks, but Ms. Wilma, Doug, Sue, and Toot each held a drip torch. Tony gave us each a mask and torch, and then pulled a backpack of water onto his own back.

"I'm going to check on Roy and the perimeter," Tony said, leaving us to work our way across the field, setting the ground on fire.

When you're walking through that much smoke and flame, it starts to take on a life of its own. The fire never rose above my knees, but the smoke hung in towers, swirling toward and away from me with dizzying speed. As the sky darkened, the ground glowed, and everything about dripping flames across that expanse of brown field felt ominous and strangely heavy. I started thinking about what might happen if Mr. Lowe and the stepdaughters had succeeded in wresting their aging parents from their beloved winter getaway. Tony and PJ, who'd lived on the island for almost twenty years, might lose their home if Horne Island developed into a golf community. Ms. Wilma and Roy would be uprooted as well. Not only did she work for the family, but she'd lived with them her whole life. Wilma's father had worked for the Leigh family when they owned property on Hilton Head. Horne was like home to Howard and me as well. Howard had spent thousands of hours in those woods, on his own and with the Leighs or some other company. Developing Horne Island would be a shame. I knew the Leighs wouldn't last forever, but selling it out from under them—and filling it with houses—would bring a tragic end to a time of our lives I knew we'd all cherish. As I swept my flaming metal canister back and forth across the grass, the realization that this could be our last spring burning settled over me like a cloud of smoke.

It took the five of us all afternoon and long into the evening to cross the field. As the flames burned themselves out behind us, we all gathered along the road before heading out for the night. Each of us, blackened with soot and filth, drank a celebratory Budweiser for another field burned. The beer felt cold and prickly on my dry throat. Ms. Wilma and Doug abstained, but the rest of us all drank several gulps before speaking.

"I wonder how things be back at the house," Ms. Wilma said to no one in particular. She drew glances from us all.

"Hard to say," Tony said. "Mr. Leigh hasn't ordered Ann and Zada out of Riverside Village yet, so maybe he's not as mad as we think."

"I thought he told those girls to pack up their things from the Indigo house," Ms. Wilma said.

"I'm not sure they had much over there," Tony said, rocking back on his heels.

"What about Mr. Lowe?" Howard said. "I wonder if he's packed up his satellite real estate office. He was all set up out on Indigo."

"That's what I heard," Tony said, laughing. "Can you believe the nerve it would take to sell an island out from under a man like Leigh?"

"I never would have guessed it myself, coming from Mr. Lowe," Howard laughed too.

"Well regardless, I hate knowing they'd coordinated all this behind everyone's backs," I said, a little worried that Mr. Leigh might actually consider developing the place. "That's just crazy."

"Speaking of crazy," Howard said, "where'd Roy end up?"

Ms. Wilma inhaled a sharp breath and said, "Where is he?" Her instinct to panic, I knew, had been hardened into her over many years of parenting someone like Roy.

I saw something flash across Tony's eyes as he looked from Howard to Ms. Wilma. "Don't worry about ol' Roy. I'm sure he'll turn up."

"Did you see him leave?" Howard pressed, more with concern than suspicion.

"No I didn't see him leave," Tony said, crushing his empty beer can in his fist. "But I know he's fine. He called me earlier. Anyways, we need to get back."

Howard and I loaded into Tony's Jeep. Ms. Wilma, who had to be exhausted after such a long day, climbed into the passenger seat of Toot's truck. Doug climbed over the tailgate in two long steps and then hoisted Sue up. They sat against the cab. Inside the Jeep, with the back seat to myself, I pulled off my hat and rubbed my eyes. The flaming ground receded into the background as we drove the Evening Trail. I wished I didn't have a boat ride across the river between myself and my bed, but it would feel good to get the fresh air after so many hours in the fire. No one said a word on the ride, and we were all so tired and stinking of smoke by the time we got back to the house that we said goodnight and barely another word before parting ways. No one noticed the horse pasture gate hanging wide open.

Martha C.

February 17, 2001

••••••

THE FOLLOWING MORNING I WOKE UP EARLIER THAN I wanted to. After burning, sleeping in seemed earned, but something got me up before dawn. I fixed a pot of coffee and took a cup out to the porch. The sun was just starting to light up the eastern sky. Thin veils of smoke still rose from Horne Island across the water. An egret flying in the distance like a white flag swooped down to the marsh and disappeared in the grass. Nothing I could see suggested this day would change all our lives. Then I heard the phone ring inside the house.

Howard answered in the bedroom on the second ring. Minutes later he was standing before me, buttoning his shirt in a rush.

"Mr. Leigh's missing," he said. His hands shook as he worked on his buttons. I sat there with my coffee watching him. "That was Tony. He found the pasture gate open first thing this morning; the mules are gone. And Mr. Leigh wasn't in his room."

"What do you mean he wasn't in his room?"

"I don't know. Tony said his Jeep was there when we all got back last night. Now it's not there. Nobody's seen him since dinner."

"Well, should I come too?" I knew as soon as I asked that

I should. I pulled on a pair of jeans and brushed my teeth, and we left the house fifteen minutes later.

The water on the Chrystal River shined like glass in the sunrise. I often worried about Mrs. Leigh getting confused and wandering off. Mr. Leigh wasn't the sort of man you worried about. He was so energetic and full of life, always in good health, but he was also in his eighties. I told myself that I shouldn't worry until we had reason to, and probably by the time we got across the river, Mr. Leigh would be there to greet us, wondering what all the fuss was about. Howard and I didn't say much on the ride, but I knew he was probably telling himself not to worry too. The river was quiet—everyone in town still sleeping. The boat motor whirred as we sped across the river and through the creek.

My worries, however, turned out to be warranted. We docked our boat at the main dock on Horne. The front of the house stood quiet and I wondered if Mrs. Leigh was even up yet. We walked around back and found Tony getting into his Jeep.

"What's going on?" Howard asked.

Tony turned to face us, his brow in a tight furrow. "Hey."

"Any word?"

"Afraid not. No sign of him at all. Roy found the horses, but the mules are missing. I'm heading out now look for him"

"I'll ride with you," Howard said, already heading for the passenger side.

"Frannie's inside," Tony said to me as he closed the driver door. As he started the Jeep and drove off, I said a prayer and walked inside the back door.

Inside the kitchen, Frannie was cutting biscuits. "Oh, Ms. Martha," she said, her hand shaking unnaturally. "Come on in. There's coffee in the pot."

"Is Mrs. Leigh up yet?" I asked, pouring my coffee.

"Not yet. Ms. Wilma's just fixin' to get her."

"So did anyone see Mr. Leigh take his Jeep out last night?"

"No, ma'am," she said, pressing the cutter into the thick dough. "Most everyone was out burning. Ms. Ann was staying here, and she said she'd put Mrs. Leigh to bed, so I went home. Mr. Leigh was reading in the living room when I left. This morning, I come over early to start my dough, and notice Mr. Leigh's Jeep is gone."

I sat down at the table with my coffee while she talked.

"Then Roy come in a few minutes later, like he always do at that time for coffee, but he's in a panic over the pasture gate. He found two horses alongside the road and the mules are gone. I'm in here, carrying on like usual, and it's like the world outside this kitchen is all mixed up."

"Where's Ann now?"

"She still in bed, as far as I know."

For almost an hour, I sat at the table while Frannie worked. She was a master in the kitchen, feeding the Leighs and their company, and often everyone else on the island too, with some of the best southern cooking you could eat. She chopped piles of carrots, celery, and potatoes for stew while I focused on the tapping of her knife on the cutting board instead of my fears. We chatted when we managed to think of something besides Mr. Leigh's whereabouts. As the minutes ticked past, I started hoping they'd last forever because I was sure bad news was coming. If Mr. Leigh took off in his Jeep in the middle of the night, any number of terrible fates could have befallen him.

Ms. Wilma had Mrs. Leigh set up at the dining room table for breakfast at 8:30. When she came into the kitchen to fix her plate, Frannie was pulling the biscuits out of the oven.

"Any sign of them yet?" she asked, nodding a greeting to me.

"Not yet," Frannie said.

"How's Mrs. Leigh this morning?" I asked.

"Oh, Mrs. Leigh's fine. I just hope her husband turns up."

Just then, I heard a Jeep pull into the yard. It was Tony and Howard. Mr. Leigh wasn't with them, which gave me a sinking feeling in my chest. Mr. Leigh wasn't with them.

Tony and Howard exited the Jeep and walked slowly up to the house. They weren't hurrying. When they came in the kitchen, Howard was shaking his head.

"It's not good," Tony said. "Mr. Leigh is dead. He died. We found him."

Frannie and Ms. Wilma cried out and embraced each other. I stood up from my seat and hugged Howard, burying my head in his chest. They'd found him on the far side of where we'd been burning. His body was burned up pretty bad, but they were sure it was him because his Jeep was parked nearby. The way the vehicle sat, Tony said it looked like he pulled off in a hurry, maybe saw the fire getting out of control or something and pulled off to stop it. His body wasn't far from the Jeep, maybe twenty yards or so, like maybe he walked out there and something happened or the smoke overtook him and he fell and didn't get back up. Hearing them describe the scene, I imagined the worst. Mr. Leigh out there suffering, needing help—it was too awful.

"I better go wake Ms. Ann," Wilma said when she'd pulled herself together. Tony called the police. I spent the next several hours in the numb state that always seems to come with tragedy. I heard Ann wailing from her room, but it quieted down after a few minutes. Ms. Wilma said Ann was going to call her siblings and she wanted to be alone.

The police and coroner came. I watched from the windows as they carted what was left of Mr. Leigh, all zipped into a dark bag, on a stretcher past the house and down to the dock. They loaded him on the boat and took him away. I sat with Mrs. Leigh most of the day, and although I'm not sure she knew what was happening, she was always a little less animated when Mr. Leigh wasn't around. I knew she'd miss him.

Late in the afternoon, Howard and I took the boat back across the river and went home. Howard had been there when the coroner and sheriffs inspected the scene, and he'd been quiet all day. I heated up leftovers for dinner, not that either of us was hungry. Frannie had cooked all day, keeping herself busy and everyone fed at once. But Howard and I sat down at our kitchen table together anyways.

"So do you want to talk about today?" I asked him, unfolding my napkin and laying it in my lap.

"I don't know, Martha." Howard put his head in his hands for a minute. "I just can't figure out what he could have been doing out there all alone like that."

I didn't say anything, just watched him and waited for him to say what he needed to say, which wasn't much. Seeing an old friend dead and in such a terrible state troubled him as it would anyone. "But you know what else I can't figure out?" he said.

"What's that?"

"Well, at the scene, there was Mr. Leigh's Jeep parked on the side of the road, and the tracks in the dirt leading up to it. But there was another set of tracks in the dirt that looked just as fresh."

"You mean like there was another vehicle there?"

"I don't know, but it sure looked like it. This other set was just as big and it looked like they pulled off the road and then pulled back out."

"Well, could Tony or someone made those tracks when we were out burning last night?"

"Maybe, but I don't remember anyone driving out that way. As far as I can remember, we were all driving on the other side."

I thought about what he was saying for a moment, and then asked what the police had made of it.

"I'm not sure they even noticed, to tell you the truth," he said. "Hell, I don't know how I noticed it myself. But there was a second set of tracks, and the more I think about it, the more I believe there was another vehicle there. If not at the same time as Mr. Leigh, then pretty close to it."

March 5, 2001

⁓⦉⦊⁓

Mr. Leigh's death cast a shadow over Horne Island. The day after finding his body, Roy found the mules. When Mr. Leigh left in his Jeep that night, he must not have closed the gate behind him. The mules wandered down to the river on the bottom end of the island. The marsh was wide there, and exposed at low tide. The mules must have walked down into the marsh to get a drink from the river and gotten themselves stuck in the pluff mud. When the tide came back in, hours later, they drowned. When Roy found them, their tawny bodies were bloated, covered in fiddler crabs, and stinking of death. Mr. Leigh loved those Belgian mules. Tony had gone all the way to Kentucky to pick them up for him and they were such pretty and good-natured animals. They'd been pulling the hunting wagon for years, and finding them like that, after who knows what they went through stuck out there in the mud, made everything seem worse.

After two nights at her mother-in-law's place in Savannah, PJ came back to Horne Island. Then Cameron and Chris came into town that week for the funeral. The four children spent the week going through Mr. Leigh's things, divvying it up amongst them. Mrs. Leigh couldn't do it herself. The service was a small family affair, held at the Church of the Cross. Mr. Leigh was buried on Horne Island under a towering live oak on the top end of the island, near enough to his dove fields and overlooking the marsh.

Afterward, Cameron and Christopher returned to their respective homes, Zada went back to New York with Ann, and Mr. Lowe, Doug heard, was renting a place in town. Doug was always playing the video slot machines at the gas station downtown. Anytime you went in there, the same three people would be lined up along the counter, working those machines: a guy who ran a wrecker, a businessman who always dressed in a suit and looked like he was supposed to be at work, and Doug. Nobody ever paid Doug any mind, but he sure found out what was going on around Riverside Village sitting in the gas station.

I had come across with Howard that morning because PJ needed to talk to me. She was moving out, she said when she called, taking Jennifer and renting a place in Savannah. When I asked what for, she said it was a long story and asked me to come help her pack. The past two weeks had been so hectic with people coming into town and the funeral, we'd hardly had a chance to talk. I wondered if she'd finally caught Tony cheating—she'd always suspected him of that. We all did. But Tony was sly and never got caught. If she was packing up and leaving, maybe she'd actually got him this time. After docking the boat, Howard and I walked up to the yard. He'd be out in the fields with Tony most of the day, which was probably why PJ chose that day to pack.

I knocked on her back door at just before nine and then let myself in. The property manager before Tony built PJ and Tony's house. The man showed Mr. Leigh a set of plans, which Mr. Leigh approved before leaving for New York, and then built something completely different while Mr. Leigh was away. With six bedrooms and bathrooms, it was more house than most people needed.

PJ called from her bedroom when she heard me come in. I found her piling clothes, pulled in armfuls still on their hangers from her closet, into a deep cardboard box.

"This week just keeps getting worse, doesn't it?" she said, pulling the last stack of hung clothing and stuffing it as far down in her box as it would go.

"I'll say." I wanted her to tell me what she needed to tell me when she was ready, so I didn't ask her what was going on. Instead I waited, listening.

"You won't believe what Cameron told me yesterday." PJ was sullen and puffy-eyed. She wasn't wearing any makeup and had a wad of tissue sticking out of the front pocket of her jeans.

"What did she say?"

"She said the autopsy results showed Mr. Leigh died of head trauma—not a heart attack or stroke or anything like that."

I expected her to tell me something about her husband. Or perhaps I wanted it to be that instead of more bad news surrounding Mr. Leigh's sudden passing. "What kind of head trauma?"

"I don't know."

"Like he got hit with something?"

"Yeah, in the back of the head. He had a big dent in his skull. It killed him."

"Oh, that's awful," I winced. "I wonder what that means."

"I just feel terrible for the kids," she said. "Cameron was a mess when she left. Ann and Zada were still weird, but, I don't know …everything feels so different. I can see it in everyone. Nothing feels right without Mr. Leigh here."

I felt it too—a surreal feeling like any minute I'd wake up and everything would be back to normal. PJ started pulling shoe boxes off the top closet shelf and stacking them into another cardboard box. I realized I was just standing there watching her and asked, "What can I pack?"

"You could start emptying those drawers. I have suitcases under the bed. Just throw everything in there and I'll sort it out later."

"Have you heard anything about what everyone will do?" I opened the suitcase at my feet and pulled open PJ's top drawer. "Do Frannie and Mrs. Wilma think they'll stay?"

"Well that's the other thing." PJ raised her eyebrows. "Cameron told me Mr. Leigh's will had Wilma and Roy in it. I didn't ask her for specifics, but she said they'd be taken care of whether or not they still had jobs."

"Wow," I said. "That's good news."

"Good news for everyone except Ann and Zada."

"What do you mean?" I pulled open the second drawer.

"Oh, you know how Ann is. Everything's about money. She just doesn't like to see her slice is a little smaller because a few extra people showed up for pie."

I laughed and pulled out a stack of jeans. We were both quiet for a while as we worked. As I transferred her things out of the dresser, I thought about the time I knew PJ and I would be good friends. It was years ago, before the girls were born, around the time they first came to Horne Island. Tony was always active in the horse-trading business, and he and I had a mutual acquaintance in a horse trader everyone called Uncle Larry. I knew Uncle Larry because he and I went in together on a racehorse named Super Boner Flash. So one Saturday, PJ, Tony, Howard, and I were driving down to visit Uncle Larry for the afternoon in Valdosta, about two hours southwest of Riverside Village. The plan was to drive down for the afternoon and come back that night. So we all rode in Howard's old dually, and on the way we stopped at a local hunting store. Howard and Tony bought all kinds of stuff, and they stuffed it all in the toolbox in the bed of the truck. So when we got to Uncle Larry's, he said he was going to a horse show for the night and asked Howard and Tony to go with him. Now, none of us packed clothes, but Uncle Larry said he'd bring Tony and Howard back to Riverside Village, and they'd just bought shirts at the hunting store so they had something clean to put on in the morning. So they went to the horse show, and PJ and I drove home in the dually. That was the first time she and I had ever spent much time together, and a long car ride is a great way to get to know someone. She and I had such a good time. We pulled into a Burger King and parked next to this fancy little Rolls Royce. The car owner was sitting inside it, and when we climbed down out of the dually, he gave us such a funny look that PJ and I laughed about it all the way home. She has a wicked, contagious laugh and once you get her going, she can't stop. The funniest thing was, when we got home, we opened up the toolbox on the dually and found the clean shirts they intended to wear to the horse show. They had to wear the same clothes all weekend. How long ago that seemed now. PJs dresser probably hadn't been emptied since she moved out here as a newlywed, and I hated the idea of her leaving like this. I'd filled two suitcases before I worked up the nerve to ask her where she was going to stay.

"I found a little apartment in Savannah near work," she said, sighing. "To tell you the truth, it will be nice not to have to commute all that way."

"So do you want to tell me why you're going?"

"Martha," she looked at me. "Tell me, do you know anything about Tony and another woman?"

"All I can tell you is what I've seen with my own two eyes," I said. I'd heard the rumors, same as she had. I couldn't tell her any more than what she'd already heard from someone else. "I've never seen Tony with another woman."

She looked at me for a moment, and then her gaze fell to the floor. Her entire closet full of clothes was now contained in two cardboard boxes and three pieces of luggage. "I appreciate that, Martha. But I don't think that's changed my decision to leave."

I didn't say anything. She fidgeted with the edge of her box.

"He had a woman out here the night y'all were burning—the night Mr. Leigh died. I know he did because I found another woman's earrings on my nightstand when I got back. He tried to tell me they were mine."

Her voice wavered as she spoke. I hated to see her go, but I also knew I wouldn't stay if our situations were reversed. I didn't know what to say, but I had her and Jennifer all packed up by midafternoon.

"It's not like I'm moving far away," she said as we were saying goodbye. Toot was waiting for her at the service dock to shuttle her across. And I figured Howard would be done with whatever he was up to by then.

"I know it," I said, hugging her as tight as I could. "I'll see you in Savannah."

I was walking across the yard from PJ's, looking for Howard to see if he was ready to leave yet, when I noticed the county sheriff's boat on the creek. When the white boat coasted up to the dock, a uniformed officer grabbed on and tied up the bow while another uniformed officer jumped ashore and tied the stern. Minutes later, the two of them, accompanied by two other gentlemen in street clothes—detectives, I assumed—were walking toward the house. I slipped in the back door, through the back rooms and kitchen and into the living room just as a firm and authoritative knock came at the door. Ms. Wilma looked up at me from her dusting with a questioning look.

"It's the sheriffs," I half-whispered. "I saw them coming in on their boat."

Ms. Wilma dropped her duster. Without another word we both walked to the door and she pulled it open.

"Good afternoon, ma'am. Ma'am," one of the men in street clothes said, acknowledging both Wilma and me with a purposeful nod. He removed his aviator sunglasses and tucked them in the collar of his blue polo shirt. The three others stood behind him like pillars. I thought I recognized the two in uniform from the day they came for Mr. Leigh, but I couldn't tell. "We're with the sheriff's department," he produced his badge in a fluid motion, as if he'd done so a thousand times, and then tucked it back away. "I'm Detective Mike Reynolds, and this is my partner Detective Jones and my associates Sergeant Williams and Officer Mace. We're here in regards to the death of Mr. Andrew Leigh."

"Yes, sir," Wilma said. "How can I help you?"

"Yes, ma'am. Can anyone drive my fellow officers and I to the site where Mr. Leigh was found on the morning of February 17?"

"Yes, come in and sit down. I'll go out back and find Howard or Tony," I said. Wilma and I stepped aside and the officers entered the house. They didn't come further than the foyer and I left them to find someone out back in the yard. When I came back in with Howard a few minutes later, they were all standing where I left them.

"I can take you out to the field," Howard said to the officers. "Come with me."

The officers nodded and followed him out without another word. Howard drove the officers to the place they'd found Mr. Leigh. They didn't say much, but Howard gathered that, although at first Mr. Leigh's death looked like an accident, the autopsy didn't reveal anything to suggest he suffered a heart attack or stroke or any other natural cause of death. His lungs weren't blackened with smoke, the police said, which suggested he was dead before the fire reached him. When Howard asked what exactly they were looking for, or what they hoped to find after two weeks had passed, they said they weren't sure what they were looking for aside from clues to what might have happened that night. Howard pulled his Jeep off the road at the scene and they all unloaded. Detective Reynolds directed each officer to a quadrant of the field and the officers spread out, searching the ground.

"Is there anything I can do to help?" Howard asked Detective Reynolds.

"Were you here the night Mr. Leigh died?"

"I was. We were on the other side of this field, burning the brush."

"Who was with you that evening?" Detective Reynolds pulled out a small notebook from the back pocket of his blue jeans and flipped it open.

"Well," Howard said. "My Martha and I were there. Ms. Wilma Chester, Doug Smith, and Toot—Tim Marshall— were working the field too. Roy was there. And Tony, the property manager."

"Did you notice anything strange that evening? Notice any activity happening on this part of the field?"

"No sir," Howard said. "We came out, burned the field, and were all back at the house by 9:00 or so. Well, all except for Roy. He didn't come back to the house with us then."

"Roy Chester?"

"Yes, sir. Tony sent him on an errand, I believe."

"An errand?"

"Yes, but I'm not sure where." Howard shook his head.

"And the morning the body—Mr. Leigh—was discovered, did you notice anything strange that morning?"

"Other than the fact that Mr. Leigh was missing?"

"Well, yes. When did you find out he was missing?"

"I was at home with my wife when Tony called. It was early—five or so—and he said Mr. Leigh and his Jeep were missing. Martha and I came across on the boat and learned that the gate had been left open and some of the horses got out."

"The gate was left open?"

"Yes, sir. Someone must have left it open the night before. Roy didn't put the horses up because we were all out burning that night. He left them out for the night. But someone must not have known that or didn't realize and left the gate open. Mr. Leigh left it, I assumed."

"Anything else stick out about that morning?"

"Yes, in fact. I noticed there was a second set of tire tracks near where Mr. Leigh's Jeep was parked. The police took pictures of them that morning—at least I thought they did."

"Like in this picture?" The officer sifted through some papers he'd pulled from his back pocket and produced a photograph of the ground.

"Yes, you can see it right there. I could see where Mr. Leigh's Jeep had pulled up. But there was another set that pulled in right over here." Howard walked to where he'd seen the tracks. Now there were tracks everywhere, several sets, from everyone who'd been there since. He pointed at the ground. "You can't really see them now, but there were tracks that pulled in right here."

"Look at this, Reynolds," the other detective called.

When Howard and Reynolds walked to where he was standing, Detective Jones showed them an old masonry stone exposed in the field. A dark stain blotted one corner. Reynolds knelt down and Jones took a picture of the stone. "We'll have to test that stain, but this could be the cause of the deceased's trauma," Reynolds said. "He could have fallen and hit his head on this stone."

"So he tripped and fell?" Howard asked.

"Not exactly," Reynolds said, standing back up. "Mr. Leigh's injury was on the back of his head, which suggests either he was hit in the back of the head while standing, or something…or someone…pushed him from the front and caused him to fall backwards."

"But his body was found over there," Howard said, pointing to the place where they found him.

"Yes, it was."

"So could he have gotten up and stumbled across the field before the blow killed him?"

"I don't think so," Reynolds said, watching Howard. "According to the coroner, a blow to the head like this is not the sort of injury someone can get up from."

"So how did he get across the field?"

"That's what we're hoping to find out."

The detectives took hundreds of pictures, collected dirt samples, and searched the whole area. One of the uniformed officers found a scrap of silk fabric caught on a tree branch. The other one came walking out of the burned field with an empty beer can and a dog whistle, which Howard recognized as Roy's. Each bit was bagged and labeled and noted in Detective Reynolds's notebook. They searched out there for three hours. Then Howard brought them back to the house and they photographed and inspected the tires of every vehicle on the island, none of which seemed to match the second set in the photo.

"Are you sure we've seen every vehicle present on the island at the time of Mr. Leigh's death?" Reynolds asked Howard after he'd assured him twice already.

"I believe so, yes," Howard said. "The only other Jeep that was on the island at that time belonged to Mr. Leigh's stepdaughter Ann. But I believe they took it off the island earlier that day."

"Any idea where that Jeep is now?"

"No. Probably Ann took it when she left."

"Thank you for your help," Reynolds said. "We'll be in touch."

I could tell the events from that day were still troubling Howard when we sat down for dinner at home. After the police left, we came back across the river and he didn't say a word about what was thinking. Sitting across from him now, over plates of leftover fried chicken, he sighed and finally broke the silence.

"I just don't know what to make of it, Martha."

"I suppose no one does."

He ate a few bites of his chicken and pushed around his pile of coleslaw with his fork. "You know if they think someone killed Mr. Leigh—and I believe they think that— then they're going to want to question everyone."

"Well that's fine, if that's what they need to do. It's not

like anyone did it."

"But someone did do it—that's the problem. Someone pushed Mr. Leigh and then dragged his body into the fire."

"I meant it wasn't anyone we know."

"Then who was it?"

I didn't say anything for a minute. The thought of someone intentionally hurting Mr. Leigh frightened me—that it could have been one of our own was unthinkable. "Howard, you know people are always sneaking over there. Remember that time I was up in the deer stand and almost shot that vet from Hilton Head because he was creeping around in the woods and wasn't supposed to be there? Just because we were the only ones on the island that we knew about, doesn't mean there wasn't someone else."

"I don't know, Martha. I just can't shake this bad feeling I have. I keep thinking about Roy disappearing that night. And then one of the sheriffs found Roy's whistle in the field."

"Well that could have been from another time. You don't think Roy had something to do with this, do you?"

"No, I don't. Not at all. But I don't know where he went that night or what he and Tony are up to. I know he didn't do it, but if everyone says he's the only one that wasn't where he was supposed to be, it could be bad."

"Howard, I'm sure there's a perfectly good explanation for where he was."

"I'm sure there is too. But I'm not the one that needs convinced."

March 6, 2001

HOWARD HAD BEEN RIGHT ABOUT THE POLICE COMING back. The detectives were on Horne Island first thing in the morning the next day, questioning Roy about his whereabouts that night. No one could say where he was for sure. As far as any of us knew, he just disappeared from the field. I heard about the detectives from Ms. Wilma later when I was fixing Mrs. Leigh's hair. She had Mrs. Leigh set up in the kitchen as usual, but Frannie had gone on errands in town so it was just Wilma and me in the house that day with Mrs. Leigh. After bringing Mrs. Leigh into the kitchen, Ms. Wilma started telling me what she knew about the detectives.

"Howard said he thought they'd be back, but I didn't expect them so soon," I said, setting Mrs. Leigh up under the dryer.

"Yes, ma'am. First thing this morning they were back out here snooping around, asking questions."

"What kind of questions did they ask?"

"Oh, all kinds of questions. But they weren't asking me. They were here to talk to Roy." She sunk into one of the kitchen chairs, folding and refolding a dusting rag she had pulled from her apron pocket. The long afternoon sun shone through the kitchen windows and cast a shadowy glow on Wilma. She almost looked ten years older than she had a week before. Ever since the questions about Roy and his mysterious errand started rising to the surface, she'd been engulfed in a sea of stress and worry. "They kept that boy talkin' for over an hour," Ms. Wilma said. "And they said they might be back to talk to him more. They talked to Tony again too."

"So what did they tell them? Where did Roy go?"

"They told them he'd gone off to pick up PJ; he said he left the field that evening because PJ needed a ride home after staying at her mother-in-law's place. Tony said that's what he told the detective too."

"Well, he couldn't have been picking up PJ because she didn't come back until the next day, after Mr. Leigh was found."

"I know," she said. Her brow was tightly knit with concern.

"Maybe they thought she was coming back then and she didn't?"

"I don't know about that. I know she mad; but I don't know if she wasn't where she supposed to be."

"So do you believe Roy went to pick her up?"

"I want to believe him. I told him no good could come from lying to the police, especially for something as serious as this."

"Did you say anything to Tony?"

"Now you know as well as I do that nobody can say anything to Mr. Tony."

"Well if those two are lying, they're just making themselves look guilty. Why aren't the police pursuing other leads?"

"They might think they don't need to. Maybe they haven't got any other leads to follow. And that Detective Reynolds was the same officer that investigated Roy's trafficking charge last year. Maybe he got it out for Roy now." Her voice wavered as she said it, and her eyes filled with tears. I couldn't imagine her fear. If Roy were put away for murdering Mr. Leigh, she'd lose everything, including her son. She dabbed at her eyes with the dusting rag and sniffled.

"Well, they have to have something. Roy didn't do it." A hot tide of anger surged in me. I tried to hide it, though, knowing Wilma needed me to be strong. "They're building a case against an innocent man while the real killer is still out there somewhere, maybe fixin' to hurt someone else."

"I know that. I keep tellin' myself the truth will come out. But if he ain't tellin' the truth, then I worry he got somethin' to lie about."

"What makes you think he's got something to lie about? Is he still hanging around with Barbara?"

"I haven't seen her comin' around so much, but that don't mean nothing. And he must have some reason to lie—otherwise he should just tell the truth. And you and I know he ain't done that yet."

"Now, Ms. Wilma, you can't let your imagination get carried away. It's no use worrying about something you can't control."

"Oh, Ms. Martha, I wish I could do that. I wish I could." She put her head in her hands and rested her elbows on the table. The dusting rag she'd been worrying sat in her lap. "I better stop gabbing and sweep," she said after a moment. Then she stood, excused herself, and left the kitchen. I heard the muffled sound of the vacuum whirr to life through the walls of the house and picked up the phone on the wall by the pantry. I dialed the number PJ had given me for her apartment in Savannah, when her answering machine picked up, I asked her to call me. Then I hung up the phone and turned my attention to Mrs. Leigh.

I washed her hair and rinsed it in lemon juice. The energetic smell rose from the sink and Mrs. Leigh let her eyes fall closed as I worked. When she was washed and rinsed, I wrapped her in a towel and sat her back up. Mrs. Leigh seemed even more removed than usual since Mr. Leigh's funeral. I wanted to think, somewhere inside her, she knew what was going on. I sat next to her during the funeral and kept searching her eyes for some indication that she was lucid, saying goodbye to her husband, getting the closure and peace one is supposed to get from a funeral. But no one could say for sure. A few times I thought I saw a gleam of recognition in her eyes, but that could have been because I wanted to see it. Without Mr. Leigh, her life hadn't changed much. Her caregivers came and went as usual, and her day-to-day didn't change—we kept it the same, thinking it would make it easier on her. But maybe she didn't even know the difference. I had her out from under the dryer and was finishing her up when the vacuum went silent. A minute later, Wilma and Mrs. Leigh's caregiver came through the butler's pantry. The caregiver took Mrs. Leigh back to her room and left Wilma and I alone in the kitchen.

That's when the commotion in the yard started. Through the window, I saw Barbara stomping out of Roy's cottage with Roy trailing behind her.

"Now what's going on out there," Wilma said, standing up from her seat to get a better look. Barbara had stopped and turned to face Roy and she was pointing at him, waving her arms in the air. We couldn't hear what they were saying from inside—their shouts muffled by the walls of the house—but they were arguing about something.

When Barbara spoke, I could practically see spit flying from her mouth like venom from a snake. Wilma rushed for the door and I followed her out to the yard.

"You better not say a damn thing," Barbara yelled before they saw us coming out the back door of the house. "This is bigger than you, Roy Chester."

"Now, Barbara," Roy said. "You know they'll find out sooner or later."

"The hell they will," she spat. "Unless you snitch."

"And what if I don't? I go away for murder?"

Across the yard I saw Howard and Tony emerge from the barn, no doubt because they heard the shouting too. Roy saw them and then glanced around the yard and saw his mother and me too. They'd drawn a crowd into their private argument. Barbara's face flushed red with anger and perhaps concern that she'd let herself get carried away and said too much too loud.

"Get the hell out of here, Barbara," Roy yelled at her. "And don't come back."

"I will, Roy, I will. But you haven't seen the last of me. If you talk, I'll talk more. And that's a promise." She turned on her heels and stomped down to the dock. Her dried out, bleached hair bounced with each step. She got into her boat, flipped the bird in the direction of the house, where we were all still standing there watching her, and sped off as quickly as she could get the boat turned around. When there was nothing left of her presence but wake, we all turned and looked at Roy.

"What the hell was that about?" Tony said as he walked to where Roy was standing.

Roy adjusted the cap on his head and shrugged his shoulders. "Tony, man, I think you know what that was about."

"I'm going inside," Wilma said, leaving my side. "I'm an old woman and I can't take this kind of nonsense."

When Howard started crossing the yard to where Roy and Tony were standing, I approached too. Tony and Roy both looked at us, perhaps wondering if we could be trusted. It didn't matter by that point because everyone knew something was going on.

"She just worried if I tell the police what I was really doin' that night that she'll get in trouble."

"To tell you the truth, Roy, I'm a little worried about that myself. You know I have a job to lose—a life and home to lose—if your activities come to light," Tony said.

"Oh yeah? Well you ain't the one have the cops sneaking around, askin' questions, like they tryin' to pin a murder on you. I got a life and home to lose too."

Tony scuffed the dust with his boots.

"What in the hell is going on with you two?" Howard asked. Tony and Roy looked at him, and then looked at me.

"It ain't nothing we can talk about right now," Tony said. "Howard, if you and Martha are ready to take off, I can finish up myself. Not much more to do anyways." He turned and walked back into the barn. The three of us stood there silent for a moment. A breeze was blowing off the river that day and the trees swayed and rustled. I couldn't wrap my head around what exactly we'd just witnessed, but it was clear that Tony and Roy, and apparently Barbara too, had something they needed to hide about the night Mr. Leigh was killed.

"Y'all know I didn't do anything to hurt Mr. Leigh, don't you?" Roy said, looking Howard in the eye.

Howard and I both nodded.

"Well, no matter what happens, I want you to remember that," Roy said. Then he walked back into his cottage and closed the door.

"He may not have harmed Mr. Leigh," I said, "but he's sure doing a number on his poor mother."

"Ain't that the truth," Howard said, placing a heavy arm on my shoulders. "Let's go home."

The next morning, not long after sunrise, I was pouring my second cup of coffee when the phone rang. I heard Howard go for it in the other room, but glanced at the caller ID anyways to see who would be calling so early. When Tony's number appeared, my stomach flipped and my mind immediately went back to that morning we lost Mr. Leigh. I didn't realize I'd been holding my breath until Howard appeared in the kitchen doorway and smiled at me. I exhaled my relief.

"What did Tony need so early?"

"Ann and Zada came into town last night," he said, making his way to the coffee pot. "They made arrangements for a zoo in Atlanta to take Mr. Leigh's zebra. Tony asked if I could meet the game warden to pick up some tranquilizer darts this morning before coming over."

"They're getting rid of the zebra?"

"It doesn't make any sense to keep it around, I suppose. As mean as that animal is, I tell you what, I'll be happy to shoot him in the ass with a dart."

I laughed and took a sip of my coffee. That zebra was so beautiful it was hard to take your eyes off it, but it was the meanest animal I believe I've ever encountered. He bit and kicked at people all the time, and if a woman was on her period, she couldn't even walk by on the other side of the pasture fence without it rearing up and charging. I wasn't surprised it was one of the first things to go. "The stepdaughters are still in town?"

He nodded. "And they're set on cleaning the place out, according to Tony."

"We better hurry and get over there. Ms. Wilma will be in a fuss."

We both dressed and got ready to leave the house. When Mary was off to school, we met the game warden at the public landing across from mother's house. Calvin Espy, one of the officers who'd ticketed everyone the day they were dove hunting, was leaning up against his black DNR pickup truck. Howard pulled his truck right in next to him.

"Good morning, Mr. Smith, Mrs. Smith," Espy smiled as we got out of the truck.

"Let's hope so," Howard said, shaking his hand.

"Tony said y'all are trying to catch a zebra? Well, I've got what you need." Espy produced a brown paper bag from the front of his truck and passed it to Howard.

Howard looked inside for a second and then closed the bag. "These should do it."

"One of those ought to knock him right down," Espy said. "We use them for deer, but they're strong enough for a bear."

"That zebra is ornery, so let's hope so."

Espy nodded, but he looked like he had something else he wanted to say, but an awkward silence fell over us as we stood there. An old truck hauling a fishing boat pulled up to the boat ramp, circled around, and was preparing to back into the water. I didn't recognize the man driving, but waved to him as he passed us standing there.

"Well, Tony and I thank you," Howard said, turning to leave.

"Howard," Espy stopped him. "I just want to apologize for any hard feelings you might have about that dove hunting incident last winter."

"No hard feelings, Espy," Howard said sincerely and almost as if he was surprised by what Espy had just said. "You were just doing your job."

"I know, but Mr. Leigh was so fired up about the whole thing, I just felt I should clear the air."

"Was he?" Howard asked. We knew Mr. Leigh was furious—he'd ranted and raved all over Horne Island—but we didn't know why Espy would know that.

Now Espy looked surprised. "Oh yeah he was. I thought for sure Mr. Leigh was going to kill someone when he found out y'all had been set up."

"No one likes to be surprised on their own property," Howard said without letting on that his suspicions were being fulfilled.

"That's true," Espy nodded. "And when my boss told him who'd sent word about where y'all would be, he was madder than ever."

Howard and I exchanged looks.

"Who sent word?" Howard asked.

"Oh, you don't know? A guy by the name of Steven Lowe made the call. My boss always says we shouldn't reveal where we get our tips like that, but Mr. Leigh got it out of him. That was only a day or two before he died. Tragic thing, the whole mess." He paused for a few minutes before continuing, "Well, I need to be off. Y'all let me know how it goes with the zebra. Like I said, one of them darts ought to do it. And tell Tony I said hello." Espy's manner had lightened, as if he'd released a weight from his shoulders and was now free to go about his business unburdened. He got back in his truck, started it up, and drove off with Howard and me standing there.

"I knew it, Martha. I knew it."

"But that still doesn't make any sense to me. Why would he get himself in trouble like that?"

"He got us in trouble because if there was trouble on Horne with the DNR, Mr. Leigh would be more likely to sell it."

Howard and I got back in his truck and went around the corner to the Horne Island landing. I could almost see the gears in Howard's brain spinning as he drove. He parked and we walked together to the boat.

"So what are you going to do? About Lowe?" I asked. "I mean, what's the use of doing anything now. Mr. Leigh's dead."

"I know, Martha. I know."

March 7, 2001

⎯⎯⎯⎯⎯ ⊰⊱ ⎯⎯⎯⎯⎯

WHEN HOWARD AND I ARRIVED ON THE ISLAND, TONY was leaning on the fence, eyeing the zebra, which was eyeing Tony right back from across the field.

"Good morning," Howard called to him as we approached.

"Howard and Martha," Tony waved. "You ready to hunt a zebra? You got the darts, right?"

"We did," Howard said, holding up the brown paper bag.

Tony laughed. "I didn't know if I'd need them or not, but I believe I will. I've been at it all morning and still can't get near him."

"Well, let's hit him with a dart. Espy said one'll do the trick."

"I hope so," Tony said, shaking his head and then looking at me. "I've got PJ coming out here tonight; she says she's taking more of her stuff. I sure don't need to fight with a zebra today."

"Then I'll assume you want to do the honor," Howard said, passing Tony the darts.

"Ha, you're damn right I do."

The darts, however, weren't as effective as promised. Tony loaded one into his crossbow and shot the zebra right in the rear end. The zebra stomped his feet and kicked at the air while the three of us stood there waiting for it to fall down unconscious. Thirty minutes later, it was still pawing at the dirt and braying at anyone who got close. So Tony shot it again, landing the dart not far from the first one. Surely a second dart would do the trick. But it didn't. This went on for hours. We stopped for lunch and ate sandwiches that Frannie brought out, but other than that, we spend all day making the zebra mad. By the time I left them to go inside and check on Wilma and Mrs. Leigh, that zebra had so many darts in his butt he looked like a peacock.

I had just sat down with Ms. Wilma at the table when Ann walked into the kitchen.

"Wilma, if you have a minute, I'd like to talk to you," Ann said. She was a plain woman, dressed in jeans and a white shirt. Her graying hair fell limp around her unmade face. But she had a nervous energy that put people on edge.

"Of course, Ms. Ann. In private?"

"No, actually, I want to see what Martha has to say about this too." Ann crossed her arms over her chest and shot me a look. "I got an interesting phone call the other day from Roy's friend Barbara. In fact, that's why we came into town."

"I can only imagine what Barbara might have to say," Wilma said. She looked surprised.

"She had a lot to say, actually. She told me all about Roy receiving shipments of drugs on Barataria." Ann paused for a moment and shifted her weight, watching our reactions.

"I'm not sure what you're talking about, Ms. Ann," Wilma said.

I shook my head. My mouth had fallen open.

"Well, that doesn't surprise me, that you didn't know about it, but Barbara seemed to know a great deal. This happens a lot, it sounds like. In fact, she said that's what Roy snuck off to do while he was supposed to be burning that night Dad died." Ann walked to the big window and stared out it for a few moments. Wilma and I exchanged aggravated looks.

When Ann turned around to face us again, she said, "Barbara also said that Tony knew all about it. He was turning a blind eye while your son was trafficking drugs on my family's property."

That's when it all made sense. Roy couldn't have killed Mr. Leigh because he was doing a drug deal. He couldn't exactly offer that as an alibi to the sheriff without taking Barbara and Tony down with him. Ann didn't see it this way.

"Ms. Ann, I don't know what that woman told you, but I do know Roy never had any trouble until he started hanging around with her. Barbara is a liar," Wilma said, crossing her thin arms across her chest.

"That might be true," Ann's voice raised. "But we all know Roy wasn't where he was supposed to be that night. We all know he's been dishonest. And we know he had a motive, because if my father caught him, Roy would need to get him out of the way. Plus my father gave Roy an extremely generous inheritance package in his will. Roy had nothing to lose killing Dad."

"That's a terrible thing to say about a man who's been loyal to your family for over a decade," I said. I couldn't listen to another word.

"Martha, did Howard know anything about this?"

I didn't answer her. He'd never said anything to me, and he seemed just as confused as I was when Roy and Tony got into that argument in the yard. Ann stared at me for a few moments. I hoped she could see she took me by surprise.

"Well, we know for sure Roy can't be trusted," Ann said. "And I told the police as much." She stood there looking at

Wilma for another moment, and then turned and walked out of the room.

Wilma clutched her chest and bent forward when Ann was gone. "Oh, Martha, this is terrible."

"Now, Wilma, don't panic."

"Oh, this is terrible." She sat in one of the kitchen chairs and rocked back and forth, shaking her head.

"Wilma, Roy hasn't been arrested, which means they don't have a case against him. At least not yet. There's still time to figure out the truth."

Her rocking slowed to a stop and she took a deep breath in through her nose.

"You need to talk to Roy—convince him to tell the truth. Murder is far worse than whatever else he has going on with Barbara and Tony."

"I told him so many times to stay away from that woman."

"I know you did. But now he has to do the right thing and say what really happened."

Wilma took another deep breath and then rose from her chair. "I have to talk to Roy." She untied her apron, hung it on a hook in the pantry, and then left out the back door without another word.

I stood in the kitchen for a moment by myself, thinking about Barbara calling Ann to tell on Roy and the way she'd stormed off through the yard and turned to flip the bird in our direction. I didn't know what to do, but I knew I needed to get out of the kitchen.

I walked outside, thinking the air would help, but seeing PJ and Tony's house, where PJ no longer lived, only made me feel worse. I missed her, especially on a day like today when I couldn't walk over there, knock and let myself in, and tell her what happened. PJ always said it was too much house for her. It did have five bedrooms and bathrooms, which was more than enough space for PJ, Tony, and Jenna. And now Tony had the place all to himself—at least he would unless he could work things out with PJ.

I found Howard in a dusty corner of the barn with Toot and Doug.

"Where's Tony?" I asked.

"I think he has company," Doug snickered and nodded toward Tony's house.

"Gloria from Georgia, I believe," Toot joined in.

Their jokes, as familiar as they were, failed to lighten my mood. I felt disgusted with all the lies and cheating and underhandedness. When had our lives become consumed by so much seediness? "Isn't PJ coming today? How could he be in there fooling around with another woman when his wife is coming?"

The three of them looked at each other and then at me. They didn't have to say it—I knew Tony would be sneaking his girlfriend out of here, probably when Doug went to pick up the kids from school. PJ worked until five. Tony always had it all figured out.

"I'm going home," I said to Howard.

"All right." He seemed to realize something was wrong. "I can't head out yet. We still haven't caught that zebra and Doug wants me to take a look at the mower."

"What's he going to do about the zebra?"

"He's got the trailer parked in the field now—he's got it filled with hay, hoping the zebra will decide to walk in there. But you go ahead and take the boat."

"I believe I will."

"I'll get a ride later," he gave me a one-armed hug before I left.

I felt better as soon as I was alone on the boat. The breeze was warm and salty, and I took my time through the creek and crossing the river.

When I pulled up to the Leigh's dock on the mainland, I noticed a red Honda Civic parked by the barn. I'd never seen it there before. After tying up the boat, I walked over to look at it and saw the Georgia plates. Gloria from Georgia—this was Tony's girlfriend's car.

I thought about PJ again, about Tony trying to convince her that the earrings his girlfriend forgot on her nightstand actually belonged to her. He was over there with that girlfriend, or maybe even another one, right now. Tony had a decent heart—he didn't cheat on PJ because he didn't love her. He was just the kind of guy who wanted a wife and wanted to run around. But PJ sounded so desperate when she asked if I knew anything. And this whole time he'd been letting Barbara drag Roy into her illicit activities on Horne Island. Roy had been putting his home—his mother's home—at risk, and Tony never told him to stop.

My watch showed 3:17. If Tony was bringing Gloria back when they went to pick up the kids at 4:00, he'd only have about an hour before PJ came to catch the 5:00 boat. That's when I dug my keys out of my purse and knelt next to the front passenger tire of the Honda Civic. I unscrewed the cap on the air valve and pushed the metal center with my house key. The escaping air blew on my fingers. The afternoon sun was hot on my back, and I had to shift my weight to keep my legs from hurting. After a few minutes, the tire was flat and I started on the front driver side one.

Just when I got the key pressing the right place, I heard the crunch of footsteps on gravel come up behind me. I turned and nearly fell over when I saw someone standing over me.

"Ms. Martha, what in the world you doin'?"

"Roy, damn it, you scared me half to death." I stood up and faced him, brushing the dust off my knees.

He mouth curled into a bright smile. "It looks like you're letting the air out of the tires on Ms. Gloria's car."

I exhaled a quick laugh that admitted my guilt. "I am. He's got that woman over there in my friend's house and PJ's coming after work today. I wanted to slow Gloria down and give PJ the chance to catch him in the act."

"Well, all right then," Roy said. Then he knelt down at the rear driver side tire and stuck his key in the valve.

"Now, Roy, I don't mean to bring you into my trouble. As long as you don't rat on me, you can walk away and leave me to it."

"You won't have time to flatten all these tires if you don't have help," Roy nodded. We were both quiet for a few minutes. I was trying not to think about what PJ would think when she got here, but happy at the same time that she'd finally have her proof. Then Roy said, "Ms. Martha, do you mind if I ask your opinion about something?"

I looked at him, still crouching by the tire of Gloria's car. "Of course, Roy."

"Well, I have come to find myself in a spot of trouble. I can't say exactly what it is, but it's got me all tied up. And there are other people involved too."

I nodded but kept quiet. I didn't want to tell him what I'd heard from Ann earlier because he might not trust me.

"The whole situation is crazy, where some people want me to lie and cover up some of the trouble to avoid trouble for everyone else. But that might lead to even more trouble …bigger trouble, for me."

He stopped for a moment, adjusted the hat on his head,

and looked at me, perhaps to gauge my reaction. Roy was a thin man, shorter than Howard, but still sturdy in his build. He always wore faded jeans and a t-shirt, with a baseball cap. And he was always ready with his cell phone clipped to his waist and his whistle around his neck, except that the whistle had been missing until the police found it near Mr. Leigh's murder scene. I wanted to yell at him for not being honest, but I just held his gaze and nodded, waiting to see what he would say.

"I don't know what to do. Mom and I have been arguing about it, and it's startin' to feel like, no matter what I do, I'm gonna have problems." He stopped again. Crescents of sweat darkened his shirt. Under his faded baseball cap, his eyes looked tired.

"That does sound like trouble, no matter what," I said after a few moments. "But, Roy, do you want my advice?"

"I do."

"You have to look out for you first. And if I were you, I'd just tell the truth. Lying to cover something up for someone else is just going to make it worse."

"Tell the truth, huh? That sounds simple enough, but it won't be easy."

"That isn't always the easiest way, but it's usually the right way."

"You might be right about that, Ms. Martha. You might be right about that." He adjusted his hat again and then stood up. He moved around the car to the fourth tire and didn't say another word about what was bothering him.

We had all four tires flattened in about twenty minutes, but that wasn't fast enough. Just as I was standing up to leave, I saw the boat coming up to the dock. They were here early to pick up the kids.

"Oh, shit," I said, stepping inside the barn so fast I nearly tripped over Roy. "Here they come now."

"Oh shit is right," Roy said, wide-eyed. "Here, quick, Ms. Martha, hide in here." He ushered me toward the back of the barn and opened the creaky door of the utility closet. Inside the cramped space, which probably hadn't been cleaned out in ages, bags of dove seed were piled on the dirt floor, a broken-down washing machine sat in the corner, and a tired broom hung on the wall.

"Are you sure?"

"Yes, I'm sure. We don't have much choice now, unless you want to use some of that truth-telling when the boat pulls up and Ms. Gloria sees her tires flattened."

I laughed and gave Roy a worried look as I stepped inside the closet.

"Just wait here until I come back for you."

"Now, Roy, don't you forget about me in here," I said as he closed the door. I listened to Roy's footsteps as he walked out of the barn and back into the yard. The sound of the boat motor was muffled through the thin walls, but I heard it stop. I pressed my ear up against the wooden wall. I heard Roy call a greeting out to them, muffled voices—probably Tony and Roy—the sound of footsteps crunching on the gravel, laughter, and then a woman's voice, loud and clear, yell, "What the hell?"

I held my breath and listened harder.

"My tires are all flat," Gloria said. "Tony, now how the hell could that happen?"

"What do you mean?"

"I mean they're flat. Look."

"Well, shit, Gloria, the timing on this is just perfect," Tony said. I could hear his anger through the barn wall.

"Let me get the air compressor and damn it you better hope those tires will hold air because PJ will be here soon. I need you out of here."

I jumped and held my breath when the outside barn door opened. Then Roy said, "Let me drag it out of there, Tony. This old barn's a mess." I sighed with relief. My eyes had adjusted to the dark now, just in time to catch sight of movement in the corner near the bags of grain. I watched as a rat the size of a man's fist came crawling out of the wall and started shoveling seeds into its mouth. I wanted to jump and scream, but like Roy said, I wasn't about to tell Gloria from Georgia the truth about her tires, so I bit my fist. The air compressor hummed to life and drowned out most of the conversation. I stood and grabbed the broom off the wall in case I needed to use it against the rat. I hadn't thought about the air compressor and figured Tony would escape from this mischief without getting caught. But then I heard the faint sound of a car door slamming and the air compressor went silent.

"You're early," Tony said.

"I got off work a few minutes early and thought I could catch the school boat," a woman said. It wasn't Gloria this time; it was PJ. She'd come early. My stomach leapt, and I barely noticed that there were now two rats sharing the closet with me.

"What the hell is going on? What is she doing here?" PJ said.

"This ain't what it looks like," Tony said.

I watched the rats as they argued outside. I couldn't make out most of their words unless they raised their voices, but I knew PJ now had what she needed. I sat in that closet for almost an hour before everything outside fell silent and Roy came to the door.

"I didn't forget about you," he said.

"Ugh, I am thankful for that, Roy. There are rats in this closet."

He laughed and nodded. "You have a good evening now, Ms. Martha. I'm driving the boat home as soon as Doug's wife gets here."

I thanked him and went home. When Howard arrived almost an hour later, I had dinner on the table waiting for him.

"Did you ever catch that zebra?"

"It was the damndest thing—he walked right in the trailer as soon as no one was looking. Tony found him in there, eating the hay, and closed the door right on him."

March 8, 2001

THE RINGING PHONE DIDN'T WAKE ME UNTIL HOWARD had answered it. I was so tired I could barely make out what he was saying or who he might be talking to. But in minutes he had hung up the phone and hurried out of bed.

"What's going on?" I asked, wincing as he turned on the bathroom light and blinded me.

"Roy and Wilma are in trouble; stuck on the river," he said, the bathroom light blazing behind him. "I'm taking the boat out to get them."

"Do you need help?" I asked, processing what he was saying and what it meant. The digital clock on the nightstand read 2:37.

"I don't know yet. Roy's drunk and his cell phone reception was bad, but he was frantic and Wilma might be in danger. I couldn't make sense of half what he was saying." Howard pulled on a flannel shirt. In the dim light, he looked like he was sleepwalking.

"Maybe you should call someone, just in case. If they're stuck on the water, it could be dangerous."

"You're right," he sighed and rubbed his eyes to wake himself. "I'll call the sheriff just to let them know something's going on. You try to get some sleep."

I lay in bed listening to Howard's voice in the kitchen. "I just want to make you aware that there's a situation. I don't know what exactly is going on, but there might be trouble," he said and then hung up the phone. The house creaked as he opened and closed the door and left the house. I listened to the faint sound of his truck starting and pulling away as the clock changed to 2:51.

When Howard got to his boat at the Horne Island mainland dock, the wind was blowing and the tide was dead low. We'd been having spring tides, which made the change more extreme in both directions. The only light was the beam of Howard's spotlight, and when it swept across the marsh, he saw the broad white hull of Roy's boat, tilted to the side and stranded on the sandbar near the mouth of Snake Creek. He slowed down and coasted through the shallow water as close as he could get to the back of the boat. When he cut his motor, Howard could hear Wilma yelling.

"Ms. Wilma, it's Howard," he yelled back to her through the darkness.

"I'm stuck, Mr. Howard." Wilma's voice was dry and tired. She sounded like she was somewhere between the bottom bank of Horne Island and the boat, and there was nothing there but marsh and mud. Why had she gone in there? While Wilma called to him and praised Jesus that someone had come, Howard found Roy slumping in the drivers seat, passed out.

"Roy! Wake up."

He did. Roy jumped and opened his eyes. They were bloodshot and rolled around for a moment before focusing on Howard. As soon as Roy remembered what was going on, he got on his feet. "What are we going to do?

"First we have to get you out of that boat." This wasn't easy. Roy, who hadn't slept long enough to sober up, swayed and stumbled. Howard started his engine and pushed his johnboat as close to Roy's as he could get it, which was still about two feet away. Roy sluggishly sat on the edge of his boat and reached one leg out for the bow of Howard's. His foot made contact, but when he put all his weight on it, he slipped into the mud and landed with a groan on his side. Howard grabbed his arm and pulled him aboard.

"Are you all right?" Howard asked, still dumbfounded at the predicament he'd found them in. "You're mother's out there stuck in the mud."

"She's still stuck?" Roy slurred.

"What the hell are you doing out here?" Roy mumbled an answer, but it was clear to Howard that if Roy was this intoxicated that Wilma must have been driving the boat. And when she got hung up on the sandbar, she tried to walk from there, across the marsh, back to Horne Island for help. The tide was low, but the pluff mud was so thick on the river bottom that she'd sunk in nearly waist high. The tide would be turning soon, so Howard had to work fast. If he didn't get her out of there, she'd drown.

Then, with poor Wilma still stuck and yelling, Howard sped down Snake Creek to the service dock, which was closest to where she was stranded. He tied his boat, leaving Roy where he was, and took the anchor rope. He grabbed a board from the skinning shed on the dock. Roy's Jeep was parked there with the driver's door hanging wide open and the keys still in the ignition. Howard wondered—probably for the tenth time that night—what in the world Roy and Wilma were doing. He got in the Jeep and drove down the service road and onto a path that led to the part of the island closest to where Wilma was stuck.

When he got to the marsh, Howard yelled for Wilma and listened for her response. He'd only left her for thirty minutes or so, but she sounded grateful to hear him close. She wasn't far from shore, but he couldn't tell exactly where she was. Carrying the board and anchor rope, he stepped into the marsh and yelled for her again. He only made it a few steps when his boots started sinking deep into the oozing mud. Walking in pluff mud, which is what they call the thick, brown river bottom mud around here, is like walking in thick pudding. So Howard set the board down flat in front of him and lay down on his belly. The mud gurgled under him and he pushed with his arms on either side, sliding the rest of the way out to Wilma.

She was covered in mud and wide-eyed with panic when Howard reached her. Working quickly, he tied the anchor rope around her chest and told her to hold on, and then he slid back to the bank. By this time, Howard was exhausted and covered with mud too. He tied the other end of the anchor rope to the back of Roy's Jeep and yelled to Wilma, "Get ready."

Howard started the Jeep, put it into gear, and as gently as he could, released the clutch. The Jeep lunged slowly forward, pulling Wilma from her muddy trap. Howard put the brake on and checked to make sure she was okay. Seeing her wave, he started moving again, pulling her, through the marsh and shells, right up to the bank. When she was back on dry land, Wilma lay there panting and crying for several minutes. Then Howard helped her into the Jeep and drove her back to the service dock, where Roy was stirring to life. Wilma may have been too exhausted to berate her son for what she'd just been through because when he rushed to her and asked if she was okay, she only said, "Son, I have been stuck in the mud and drug up through the marsh. I okay tonight, but I too old for this."

"What in the world were you doing out here at this time of night?"

Wilma looked at Roy, and Roy hung his head. "Mr. Howard," Roy said after a moment. "I can't tell you all the details, but the truth is I need to get out of town for awhile."

"The police want to blame Roy for Mr. Leigh's death," Wilma looked pleadingly at Howard. She was covered in mud up to her neck and still breathing heavy.

"Y'all are running?"

"That one way to call it," Wilma said.

"Roy, don't you think it's time you tell the truth about where you were when Mr. Leigh was killed?"

"Howard, sir, you have to know I didn't hurt Mr. Leigh."

"I know that, Roy. Everyone does. But the detectives are mounting a case against you because you haven't told the truth."

Roy adjusted the hat on his head.

"You can't run, Roy, because that just makes everything look worse, like you really did it. If you get arrested, I promise I'll figure out how to get you out of it. But I can't help you if I don't know what was really going on. And I ain't helping you run."

"I ain't gonna run. At least not tonight." Roy said, and then turned to Wilma. "Mama, we need to go back to the house tonight. You should take the Jeep. Howard, will you take me back out to the boat?"

The sun rises so early that time of year, and the sky was already filling with light. Wilma went home to get herself cleaned up and Roy and Howard headed back to the sandbar. But when they got there, the boat was gone. The tide had come in a few feet by then, and the boat wasn't anchored. There was no sign of it anywhere.

"Maybe the DNR picked it up," Howard said. He'd called the sheriff before he left, so maybe they'd sent a boat to the area.

"I might prefer someone came along and stole it," Roy said.

They didn't wonder for long because as soon as the mainland dock came into view, they saw, in the dim morning light, Roy's boat tied next to the larger DNR boat. Detective Reynolds was standing on the end of the dock waiting for them.

"Roy Chester, you're just the man we wanted to see," the detective said when they approached. "You're under arrest for the murder of Mr. Andrew Leigh."

"Murder?! Now I didn't kill nobody," Roy protested.

"What proof do you have?" Howard asked.

"We have enough to take Roy in," the detective said. "First, your alibi didn't hold up. It took us a while to find her, but when we talked to PJ Jenson, she said she didn't come home that night and didn't meet you for a ride across the river. Then this morning, we come out because we hear of trouble on the river and come across your boat, abandoned. And when we go aboard to investigate, we found this." He produced a plastic evidence bag holding a smaller bag of white powder and a string. "Do these look familiar to you, Roy? I'm sure the drugs do."

"What's that got to do with Mr. Leigh?" Roy demanded.

"His daughter seems to think it has a lot to do with it. If you were running an illegal drug trafficking operation off Horne Island, you sure have a motive to kill Mr. Leigh if he discovered what you were up to. Plus this string, this whistle cord we found at the crime scene, matches the description several witnesses gave of your dog whistle." The detective replaced the evidence bag in his pocket. "This links you to the crime scene and was more than enough to convince the judge."

"Of course I'm linked to the scene of the crime," Roy argued. "I work on the island."

"Now, Roy, my job is to gather evidence and bring in the suspects that evidence points to; not judge your guilt or innocence." He puffed up his chest. "You can make my job easy, or you can make it hard. Either way, I intend to do my job this morning."

Roy looked out across the water. He was still on Howard's boat, just out of law enforcement's reach. The DNR officers, detective, and officer stood watching them on the edge of the dock.

"Howard, what am I gonna do?" Roy whispered.

"Roy," Howard said. "You remember what I said? You need to tell the truth, and the only way it's going to come out is if you go with the detective now."

"Mr. Howard," Roy said wearily, "I've got a record. Once they get me in jail, they won't care about finding the truth. I know how it work."

"Roy," Howard put both hands on Roy's shoulders and faced him. "If you go with them now, I promise to find the truth."

Roy looked at him and then closed his eyes and sighed.

"Okay?"

"Okay." Roy turned to the police on the dock and said, "I guess I'm making your job easy this morning."

"I appreciate that, Roy," the detective said.

Howard stood watching as they placed Roy in custody and hoped he could keep his promise.

March 16, 2001

⠶⠶⠶

Roy's arrest was a troubling reality and Howard believed finding the missing Jeep was essential to figuring out who might be responsible. Mr. Leigh told Tony to get the Jeep off the island when he found out Zada, Ann, and Lowe had been planning real estate deals behind his back. Tony couldn't remember who he told to take the Jeep over, and both Roy and Doug remember thinking the other one was taking care of it. Then the Jeep was gone—disappeared, as far as anyone knew, the night of Mr. Leigh's death. Whoever had that Jeep, Howard suspected, would know something. The problem was, that Jeep could have been anywhere. Howard dug out a picture of Mr. Leigh with the Jeep parked in the background and showed it to everyone he bumped into around town, asking if they'd seen it around. The answer was always the same: no. And I could see him looking for it every time we got in the car. Finally I offered to ask Mother to help. "Make a few copies of the picture and I'll give them to her. She always knows what's going on in town." I didn't actually think anything would come of it. It wasn't that I doubted Howard that the Jeep was significant, but I doubted anyone would ever find it. If the police hadn't found it, it had to be gone.

The next evening I brought mother pork chops and rice and the picture of the Jeep. She hadn't seen it, but would certainly start looking, she said. I explained the whole story to her and she agreed the missing Jeep seemed suspicious. But she was a busy woman, even at her age, and I wasn't sure how much thought she gave it.

Mother and I had just finished our dinner when the sound of sirens stirred the night. Not paying the noise much mind, I stood from her kitchen table and carried my plate to the sink. I rinsed off what was left of the rice, and had turned to clear hers when I noticed the red lights flashing at the Horne Island landing.

"What's going on outside?" I walked past mother and out the front door for a better look. She stood and followed me. The sun had gone down about fifteen minutes before. An ambulance and fire truck, I could see in the flashing red lights, were parked at the landing near the dock. I could see people moving around, passing in and out of the light, but from the distance couldn't tell who they were.

"What's going on?" Mother asked, standing behind me now.

My first thought was Mrs. Leigh, and it was probably mother's as well. "I don't know, but I'm going to call Howard."

I walked back into the kitchen where the phone hung on the wall and dialed our house. Waves of fear and sadness rushed over me every time it rang. I just didn't think, after the past six months, that I could take any more bad news. When Howard answered, I explained that something was going on down at the landing. "There's an ambulance there. Have you heard anything? It could be serious."

"I'll go check it out."

"Should I meet you there?"

"I'll let you know once I get there. It might be nothing."

"Do you need to go?" Mother was standing in the doorway when I hung up the phone.

"No. Howard said he'll call."

Mother and I sat and worried on her front porch, watching the red lights revolve and sweep across the mainland house and out over the water. When Howard arrived at the landing a few minutes after we spoke, he jogged from his truck, past the fire truck and ambulance, to the dock, where he saw Doug kneeling, looking into the boat, Gloria was standing on the barge, and three paramedics huddled around someone. From the tear-streaked and nervous look on Gloria's face, he guessed it was Tony. When he reached Doug's side on the dock, Howard saw he'd guessed right. The paramedics were doing CPR on Tony, who was sprawled out on the floor of the barge. Howard recognized one of the paramedics from around town—a young woman in her twenties, her parents lived on Oyster Street—but he'd never seen the other two. Tony lay unconscious and limp as they worked.

Doug stood up and nodded at Howard.

"What happened?"

"Oh, Howard, it was terrible," Gloria said. "He said he felt funny on the ride over, like he was short of breath, but we got here okay. Then he stood up to tie the boat and just fell back clutching his chest. It was awful. I ran up to the house and called 911 while Doug stayed with him on the boat, and by the time I got back he was unconscious." She wiped her eyes with the back of her hand. Mascara ran down her face.

"I've got a pulse," one of the paramedics, a thin young man with dark hair, said. "Mr. Jenson, can you hear me?"

Tony didn't respond.

"Pulse is still strong. Let's get him out of here." The two other paramedics—a heavy-set man in his thirties and the familiar young woman with her hair pulled in a tight bun—pulled a stretcher onto the boat and the three of them, in one smooth motion, lifted and positioned Tony's heavy body onto it.

"Where are you going to take him?"

"Hilton Head, ma'am. Are you Mrs. Jenson?" the young woman paramedic said.

"Not exactly," she said looking at Howard. "I'm his girlfriend."

"You're welcome to ride along. Anyone else can meet us there."

Howard moved out of the way as they lifted the stretcher out of the barge and hurried down the dock for their rig. Gloria followed them, hugging herself as she walked. Before following them, Howard asked Doug if he'd been on the barge too.

"Yeah, we were bringing Gloria and a load of Mrs. Leigh's old things over and he was complaining the whole way about not feeling right."

As Howard walked down the dock, he settled his eyes on the rim of the barge. The thick steel hull was covered in chipped reddish-brown paint. It wasn't a pretty vessel, but it was solid and probably impossible to sink. When he approached the front of the barge, something on the hull stopped him. He leaned in closer and saw a dent in the side of the boat that he'd never noticed before. He didn't use the barge that often and it was old and weathered, but this dent was big, almost like the boat had hit a cement piling, and it hadn't rusted over yet.

"Hey, what the hell happened here?" Howard said, pointing the dent out to Doug.

"Funniest thing," Doug shook his head. "Nobody knows what happened to it. One day it was just dented. Probably someone forgot the utility barge has been out in the river and hit it."

"When did that happen?"

"A while ago. The night of Mr. Leigh's passing in fact. I come over with the kids to go to school and found it tied up and bashed in like that."

"Well who did it?"

"Like I said, nobody knows. With everything else going on, never thought to ask."

"Damn," Howard said, turning and walking away. "Never thought to ask?"

Tony was just coming to when Howard and Doug reached the ambulance. The paramedics were switching him onto the gurney when he started moving and coughing.

"Tony, Tony," Gloria yelled when she saw him.

"Is he conscious?" Howard said, standing at the foot of the gurney. The paramedics stopped moving him to see what would happen. Tony's chest rose and fell, and then his head started moving back and forth, as if he were trying to wake up. Doug and the two other paramedics stopped what they were doing and all eyes were on Tony, who furrowed his brow, winced, and opened his eyes. His face looked pale and distant.

"Tony!" Gloria yelled again.

"Mr. Jenson," the heavy-set paramedic said. "You've suffered a heart attack and we're taking you to the hospital."

Everyone watched Tony with anticipation, as he looked at each face in the small crowd around him. Finally, he coughed one last time and spoke groggily. "Where's PJ?"

Gloria's jaw dropped and the paramedics snapped back into action, sliding the gurney into the back of the truck.

"Ma'am, if you're riding with him, I'll need you to step inside and take a seat," the paramedic said to Gloria.

Howard and Doug tried not to laugh when she shook her head and rolled her eyes, but loaded into the ambulance anyway. The paramedic closed the back doors and then took her place in the passenger seat. The lights on the ambulance were still flashing as they started the engine and backed away from the dock. Howard and Doug watched them speed off with the fire truck, lights off, following them out.

"Well, that was awful," Doug said to Howard after the ambulance and fire truck were gone and silence fell over the landing. He still looked shocked.

"No kidding. I need to go get Martha. She saw the ambulance pull in from her mother's and is probably worried sick."

"Yeah, I'm going back to Horne. I can tell everyone there and hopefully call the hospital in a while to see what's going on. Ms. Wilma will want to call PJ," Doug nodded and turned to walk back toward the dock, but then he stopped. "Hey, what's the big deal about the barge, anyway? That thing's so banged up you can hardly tell the difference."

"The police are looking for a murderer, Doug. They're trying to pin this on Roy. To me, an unexplainable dent in the barge looks like evidence."

"I know Roy didn't wreck the barge," Doug said.

"I know he didn't either," said Howard. "But someone did."

Mother and I were sitting inside at her kitchen table drinking tea when the headlights from Howard's truck flashed through the side windows. He walked through the front door a minute later with a weary look on his face.

"Is everything all right?" I asked.

"It was Tony. He's alive. But he had a heart attack."

"I just made coffee," Mother said, standing up to fix him a cup.

"What happened?" I asked.

Howard sat down and explained about Tony. And then he told us about how Tony asked for PJ when he came to. We were all relieved that he'd spoken at all. It meant he was alive and would probably live another day. But I wondered if the stress of juggling his personal affairs hadn't caught up to him. After about an hour, I called Wilma to see if they'd heard anything. They were keeping Tony at the hospital, she said. He'd suffered a serious heart attack and might need bypass surgery. Gloria, who was staying at the hospital, promised to call with an update in the morning.

"Mr. Tony run everything over here. He tells them all what to do when. I don't know what we're gonna do tomorrow," she clucked into the phone. I told Wilma to get some sleep and I'd call her early the next day.

Mr. and Mrs. Leigh loved Tony because he ran Horne Island so well. They treated Tony and PJ's daughter like their own grandchild. One summer they asked if they could dig a pond where Jennifer could swim—a simple hole in the ground so she could get wet. Mrs. Leigh insisted they put in a dock with a gazebo so she'd have a place to dry off.

"That's really not necessary," PJ told her. "A hole in the ground with some water is just fine."

But Mrs. Leigh couldn't help herself. They loved them like family. And Tony couldn't do wrong in their eyes. Every time he and PJ had problems, they sided with Tony because he never was honest with them about the other women. They thought PJ was the problem and Tony was fine leaving it that way so he could keep his benefits.

Just as I drank my last swallow of tea, Howard said, "You want to know something else? While the paramedics were taking Tony, I noticed a dent in the barge that I'd never seen before. When I asked Doug about it, he said it happened the night Mr. Leigh was killed and nobody knows how the dent got there."

"What do you make of that?" I asked, not sure what to think.

"Well, I'm not sure, but it seems like if someone were in a hurry to get away from a murder scene, they might smash the barge on a piling and take off without bothering to tell anyone."

"You know, now that you mention it," Mother said, "I saw the barge come over that night."

"You did?"

"Yes, I did. I couldn't sleep, so I was sitting out on the porch like I like to do, watching the fire smolder across the way, and I saw the barge come in. It must have been two in the morning."

Howard and I watched her wide-eyed. She seemed to be piecing her memory together as she told us about it.

"I didn't think much of it because I knew they'd be up late burning. The barge pulled up to the dock and unloaded a car or some kind of vehicle, and whoever it was drove away after ten minutes or so. They didn't stay at the landing for long."

"Well who could it have been?" I said, not expecting her to have the answer. There was no way she could have seen much more than the boat itself.

"I don't know," mother shook her head.

"I know one thing for sure," Howard said. "Someone needs to find out."

March 17, 2001

Daily operations on Horne Island fell fast into chaos without Tony or Roy there to know what was supposed to happen when. Doug and Toot knew enough to keep themselves busy, and Wilma and Frannie could hold the house together no problem. Wilma took two days off after her ordeal on the river, but she was back to work and her bruises had healed. But the vet showed up at noon and no one knew which animal he was supposed to look at and the phone in Tony's office rang all day. He wasn't expected to be out of the hospital for another week, even then, the man was having a triple bypass. He might not be well enough to work for months.

When PJ called me that evening, I was cleaning up after dinner. She said Zada and Ann should be arriving from New York anytime now and Cameron and Christopher were both coming in the following day. "They're all coming in to assess the situation and figure out what to do."

"That doesn't sound good." I scraped the last plate and set it in the sink.

"No, it doesn't."

"They'll have to sell the place. What else will they do?"

"Yes, but it's going to take a lot of work even to get to that point," she said. "They need someone to take over the day-to-day. Tony may be a dirt bag, but he ran the place well."

I shifted the phone on my shoulder as I wiped off the table. "Did you hear he asked for you on the landing while he was having the heart attack?"

"Ha! Wilma did mention that. I half-thought Doug was lying."

"Nope. Howard heard it too. He said Gloria almost died, standing there next to him, worried sick, and he comes to for a minute and looked for you," I laughed. "Can you imagine?"

"It serves them both right," PJ said, chuckling.

I knew then that my friend's marriage was really over. Her time on Horne Island was done, and perhaps ours time was running out too. What would we ever do without Horne Island?

"Listen, Wilma and I were talking, and we think Howard should come over and take over while Tony's laid up."

"You think so?"

"Absolutely. Who else could do it? Doug can barely keep the feeding schedule straight. Toot just doesn't have the energy."

"I'm sure he'd be willing to help, but Zada and Ann will have a fit about having to pay someone else."

"I'll take care of Zada and Ann. Let's go over there tomorrow. I hate being in town for St. Patrick's Day with everything going on downtown. And Jennifer needs to get a few things from the house anyways, and I prefer to do it while Tony's not around. I'll tell Frannie to count us in for lunch and we can go over together first thing after church."

"I guess it couldn't hurt to mention it to Howard. He loves any excuse to spend time out there anyways."

The next morning, right after church, PJ, the girls, and I met Doug and his wife Sue at the landing. Sue was running a few errands early that morning, and Howard wasn't coming over for another hour, so we caught a ride with them on their trip back. It was pouring down rain so heavy you could hardly see through it, so I wasn't thrilled about Doug driving. But we all loaded onto the boat in the rain and huddled under the awning. Doug drove slowly, but then he said something to PJ about Roy getting arrested and I started to wonder whether more than Doug's vision was cloudy.

"You sure blew his cover, PJ." He smiled like he didn't know how much that comment might bother PJ.

"Doug, what did you expect her to do, lie too?" Sue said, mad that her husband had said something so insensitive. "It's not her fault."

"Well, that's not what I meant," he said, "I just meant that Roy's scheme, whatever it was, had run it's course."

"It's fine, Doug. I know what you meant." PJ smiled at Sue. "I didn't even know he'd used me as a cover. When the police come knocking on the door, I'm inclined to tell the truth."

"Well, that's more than we can say for Roy, unfortunately," Doug said.

"I just feel terrible for Ms. Wilma, having to deal with all this," I said.

We were all quiet on the last few minutes of the ride. I couldn't help thinking about Wilma stuck in the marsh, almost drowning because of Roy's mess. If they hadn't gotten stuck, she'd go to jail with Roy when the authorities caught him. I was still thinking about what a mess everything had become when we pulled up to the service dock. Then Doug stepped out of the boat, slipped on the wet planks, slid all the way across, and fell into the river on the other side.

Sue, PJ, the girls, and I all looked at each other wide-eyed when we heard the splash. After a few more splashes, Doug yelled, "I'm all right." He stood up and hoisted himself back out of the water and onto the dock. Water pooled all around him. He was soaked from head to toe, and we all had a good laugh.

"It's about time something funny happened around here," Sue said, wiping tears from her eyes.

"I'm going to have to go get cleaned up before coming in for lunch," Doug said.

"I'll come with you." Sue followed him up the dock. PJ and I called our goodbyes to them and then made our way through the yard, around the house, and in through the back door.

When we walked into the warm light of the kitchen, Frannie was pulling a roasted chicken out of the oven and Ms. Wilma had a stack of plates in her arms.

"Hello, ladies," Wilma said, seeing us. "Let me take these out to the table and I'll be right back."

"We have a full house for lunch today," Frannie said.

"Ann and Zada made it in?" PJ asked.

"They did."

"There's coffee there," Wilma said, coming back into the kitchen and brushing her hands over her apron. "Have a seat there at the table. We're almost ready to serve."

This was the first time I'd seen Wilma since Roy was arrested. He was still in jail because they'd set the bail ridiculously high and Wilma didn't have the money to get him out. Wilma and I had spoken quickly on the phone since the arrest, but her thoughts could have been anywhere. And if Doug had been talking about PJ getting Roy in trouble, then Wilma could be thinking that too. No one spoke as

PJ and I fixed our coffee and sat. Worried about what tension that silence might contain, I remembered Doug and laughed. "Oh, Frannie and Wilma, you should have seen Doug fall in the water."

PJ laughed into her coffee. "I'll never forget the look on Sue's face when she heard the splash. We all looked up from what we were doing and Doug was gone," she smiled.

Wilma and Frannie smiled too and watched us as we told the story. "The second Doug put his weight on that foot, it slipped right out from under him and he didn't stop sliding until he was in the water," PJ said, wiping tears from her face.

"Oh, poor Doug." Ms. Wilma shook her head. We sat and laughed about it until Frannie and Wilma finished lunch.

Then PJ folded her hands in her lap, turned to face Wilma, and said what I knew had been weighing on her mind since we stepped into this kitchen. "You know, Ms. Wilma, about Roy. When I told the detective that Roy didn't give me a ride that night, I didn't know he was going to get in trouble for it."

Wilma shifted her weight; she was leaning against the counter, looking at PJ. "I know that," she said. "I don't blame none of Roy's trouble on you. If I blame anyone," she paused and looked over her shoulder with wide eyes, "it's Mrs. Leigh's conniving daughters. They wanted Roy put away."

"Well, I want to tell you how sorry I am that he's gotten himself into this mess."

"I appreciate that. It's not easy being Roy's mother, but you're like family to Roy and me, PJ," Wilma said. "Now let's talk about something besides my troubles." She looked at me and continued, "Ms. Martha, now is Mr. Howard going to save us from this mess Roy and Tony left behind?"

"I'd like to know that too," Frannie said. "Tony been gone two days and already nothin' gettin' done."

"Did y'all hear the vet came out yesterday and nobody know what for? I told Zada he gone charge them anyway," Wilma said, shaking her head.

"Well, I talked to him, but he didn't say yes or no. I don't think he'll believe the sisters will allow it until he hears it from them." I set my coffee cup on the table. "He should be here with the boat anytime now."

I could hear voices coming from the dining room where everyone was starting to gather.

"We best get lunch service going," Wilma said, and we all headed for the dining room.

Zada sat in Mr. Leigh's favorite spot at the head at the table; Ann was seating herself next to her. Wilma brought Mrs. Leigh in and sat her next to Zada. Doug, who'd showered and changed, was next to Ann and Sue was next to him. PJ went for the seat next to Sue, and I was pulling out the chair next to hers when Howard walked in through the kitchen.

"Aha, here he is," Zada said. "Since we're all here, this is the perfect time to talk about everything that's happened over the past few weeks. Howard, have a seat."

I knew PJ had spoken to Zada and Ann about Howard helping out, but I didn't know if they'd taken her advice. A hush fell over the table as everyone settled and filled their plates. The Leigh's dining room looked almost the same as it had the first time I saw it. Mrs. Leigh's Blue Willow China was displayed on the buffet and in the cabinet. The long, wooden table was solid but worn from years of parties and dinners. And the linens were crisp and pressed as always. Then Zada stood and welcomed everyone.

"We were going to wait until Cameron and Chris got in tonight, but with everyone here, it feels like the right time to share some important news," she said, looking around the table. We all stared back at her. Zada smiled nervously and then continued, "We know this place is like a home to you all, but with dad gone now and mom so sick, it just doesn't make any sense to maintain the house and island when no one's around to use it."

PJ nudged me under the table while Zada flipped her hair and raised her gaze to the ceiling. "I'm afraid I don't know how to say this…"

"We're putting Horne Island up for sale," Ann stood up next to her sister. And there it was, the decision we'd all expected would come eventually but hoped never would, now lay upon the table.

"Did you know about this?" I mouthed to PJ.

She shook her head. No one said a word, but Wilma, who was standing in the doorway, let her mouth fall open.

Finally, Doug spoke. "Well, Ms. Ann, Ms. Zada, that's sad news, but what are we going to do in the meantime? We've got a full-time property manager laid up sick, and for sale or not, the place has to be maintained. We just can't do it on our own."

"As much as we hate to incur any additional expense," Ann said. "With Tony and Roy both absent, we realize we need someone here to get the place sold and cleared out."

Wilma, who was setting a bowl of green beans on the table, looked at Ann like Ann had two heads. "*You* realized?" Wilma said, not quite under her breath. "More like everyone else told you."

Ann looked sharply at Wilma, who set down the beans and headed back to the kitchen without another word. Then

Ann said to no one in particular, "She should keep her worries where they belong, on her son and his illicit activities."

"PJ mentioned that, Howard, you might be willing to help," Zada said, looking from her sister to Howard, who was next to me shoving a biscuit in his mouth.

He nodded to acknowledge Zada's question while chewing and swallowing. I couldn't tell if he was taking his time while he thought about his answer or if she'd genuinely caught him with his mouth full. Everyone watched as he took a gulp of his tea and finally spoke. "Nothing pains me more to see Horne Island sold to a stranger." He looked around the table and settled his eyes back on Zada. "I want to spend as much time here as I can before it's gone. I'll help however I can."

Zada's shoulders fell and she sighed. "That's wonderful," she said, bubbling with relief. "Thank you. We'll settle the particulars after we eat, but I'm sure we need to you to start right away. PJ, would you mind taking Howard up to Tony's office? You probably know his system better than anyone. I know Doug said he couldn't make much sense of it yesterday."

"That's true; just looked like a mess to me," Doug said.

"That's no problem at all," PJ said. "We can walk over there as soon as lunch is finished."

Howard nodded and took another drink of his tea. Wilma returned with another basket of biscuits, which she set on the table next to Zada.

"Oh, I'm so glad that's settled," Zada said, reaching for a biscuit. "With everything that's been going on, Ann and I have just been so worried."

"With everything that's been going on, Ms. Zada," Wilma said, "don't choke on your biscuit." She turned on her heels and strutted back into the kitchen.

A flicker of annoyance crossed Zada's face. I looked around the table at everyone—everyone but Mr. Leigh. It didn't feel right sitting there without him, and it didn't feel right that the fate of his island would be settled like this. But I also knew the Leigh's children were the only people left who had any right to decide the island's future. I couldn't exactly hate them for exercising it, even if I didn't agree. The room had grown awkwardly silent.

"So how long do you and Ann plan on staying on Horne Island?" I asked Zada to break it.

"Indefinitely," Ann said.

"Well, not indefinitely," Zada explained. "As short a time as possible, hopefully. We want the place to sell, obviously. But we'll stay until we get mother moved over to Riverside Village and all settled in."

"Will we be seeing more of your friend Mr. Lowe?" Sue asked casually. "He lives in Riverside Village now, doesn't he?"

Ann shot Zada a look so fast that she dropped her fork onto her plate with a *clang*. Howard stopped chewing and watched to see what Zada would say.

Zada dabbed her mouth with her napkin and said, "He does live in Riverside Village now. He liked it here so much I couldn't get him back to New York. That reminds me, Howard, maybe you can give me a lift over to the mainland later. I have some errands to run."

"That would be fine," Howard said. He gave me a curious look and then mopped his plate with last piece of biscuit and shoved it into his mouth.

March 18, 2001

TONY'S OFFICE WAS A SMALL CORNER OF THE BARN.
One of the first changes he made as manager at Horne
was enclose and air-condition the little space. No one but
him spent much time in there, and when Howard stepped
inside it, he couldn't remember the last time he'd been in
there. Everything still looked relatively similar to when he'd
helped Tony bring the desk in from the house. Now that
desk was buried in papers and notebooks. Tony wasn't the
neatest person, and his organization methods weren't obvi-
ous to anyone but himself. There were stacks of papers and
receipts on every surface. So Howard had no idea where to
start and PJ didn't know what to tell him. She showed him
the calendar and Tony's Rolodex, and then left him to get
what she needed from her house.

Howard sat down in the upholstered swivel chair and
tilted it back. The chair squeaked painfully as he rubbed
his eyes for a moment. Then he let the chair fall back down
and started sifting through the papers. Most of it was unin-
teresting—receipts, old messages, information about horse
shows—and Howard sorted it all into piles. By the end of
the afternoon, the desk was cleared except for one small
stack, he'd made nine phone calls, and he understood every
note on the calendar. Howard, set on finishing up soon,

120   *Martha C.*

flipped through the remaining pile of papers just to make sure it contained nothing that needed immediate attention. That was when the Smith, Davis, and Bartholomew letterhead caught his eye. He recognized the name as Zada and Ann's attorneys. He remembered hearing about them when the Leigh's sold a piece of property they owned on Hilton Head because they'd raised a big stink about Ann and Zada's share of the profits. Howard pulled the letter out of the stack.

December 19, 2000

Dear Mr. Tony Jenson,

This letter is to acknowledge receipt of the property records you sent on December 3, 2000. We now request records of all operating expenses, as discussed on the phone, for the past five years. Please call with questions.

Your cooperation and prompt response are greatly appreciated.

Sincerely,

Edwin Bartholomew

Howard read the letter twice, then folded it and tucked it in the breast pocket of his jacket. He stood, turned off the light, and locked the office behind him.

Zada rode with PJ, the girls, Howard, and me back across the river when we left. It was almost five, and the river sparkled in the afternoon light. She didn't say much, just stared at seemingly nothing, straight ahead, her gauzy blouse billowing in the wind. When we'd crossed, docked the boat, and unloaded ourselves, she thanked Howard again for helping out and for the ride. Zada never said explicitly where she was going, but since lunch she'd put on a nice blouse and diamond earrings, which gave me the feeling she was meeting Lowe. I tried to remember the last time I actually saw him in person. He was supposedly staying in Riverside Village, but he disappeared from Horne Island and I couldn't recall ever seeing him around town. Riverside Village was the kind of place you bumped into people, but Lowe seemed to have vanished.

Zada strolled down the dock, across the parking lot, and into the back door of the mainland house. A minute later she emerged, carrying a set of keys in her hand, and walked back across the parking area to the barn where Mr. Leigh's Jeep had been parked since the police finished searching it for evidence. Roy drove it once in a while, but the Jeep sat unused for weeks at a time. Still, when Zada turned the key, the engine stirred to life. She backed the Jeep out of its space beside the barn and drove out to the road.

Howard watched her take a left. Then he looked at PJ and me and said, "PJ, give Martha a ride, will you? There's something I need to go see."

"What?" I said. "Where are you going?"

He was already jogging toward his truck. "I'll tell you later," he yelled back. He waved before hurrying into his drivers seat, speeding down the drive, and turning left.

"What do you think he's up to?" PJ looked at me.

"I'm sure I could guess," I said.

"Are you okay?"

I sighed. "Yes, I'm fine. I'm a grown woman; I know things change."

"That place will probably sit on the market for months. Not everyone has the money to buy an island."

"I hope you're right."

Howard drove too fast down Alljoy Road trying to catch up to her and, taking a guess, took a right on Boundary in town. When he turned, he saw the Jeep up ahead making a left at the four-way stop in the middle of town. He checked his speed twice more before reaching the stop and following Zada south on Chrystal River Road. By the time Howard had turned, Zada could have turned off any of the small side streets in the center of town. But he spotted the Jeep up ahead when he passed the Piggly Wiggly. She was driving slowly, perhaps because she wasn't familiar with the area, and heading out of town. Live oaks shaded the road, which was wooded on both sides. The wisteria vines, bursting with their heavy lavender blooms, hung in the bare trees. Howard was only a hundred yards or so behind Zada when she turned left onto the dirt drive that led to the Martins' plantation house.

The Martins bought the place about eight years before. The spacious mansion was much larger than their house in town, with property, a barn, and a stunning view of the river. Closer to the headwaters, the Chrystal River was marshier there and saw less traffic than the part downtown. When Mrs. Martin saw the property, she said she couldn't resist. But as far as Howard knew, the Martins weren't in town and hadn't been since their son got sick last winter.

Howard hit the brakes and saw the Jeep disappear into the woods as he passed the drive. He slowed down until he got to where the county was putting in the new parkway south of town, checked to make sure he was clear, made a U-turn, and doubled back to the Martins'. This time, he turned down the wooded drive.

Howard had been to the Martins' plantation house twice before. Once for a party when they first bought the place, and a second time to help Mr. Leigh and Mr. Martin when the washing machine flooded. The driveway was lined with pinewoods on both sides, and, after almost a quarter of a mile, came to the clearing on the river where the house stood. Howard drove about halfway back to the house and parked his truck as far to the side of the driveway as he could get. He knew that if Zada came back out, she'd see him. But he also knew that if he were right about what she was doing here, then she'd probably be distracted for a while. Howard wasn't even sure exactly what he'd followed Zada to find—maybe he just needed to validate his suspicions that Lowe was hiding out in Riverside Village. All this time, he'd felt in his gut that Lowe had a reason to hide.

Gravel crunched under his boots as he walked along the road to the house. When he got close enough to see the place and be seen, he stepped off the road into the woods. He crept through the brush and crouched down where he could see the yard. The house—an expansive white antebellum with four columns and a wrap-around porch—looked empty. The sun was still an hour or so from setting, and it cast a shadowy glow over the place. He didn't see anyone on the porch or in the yard. He also couldn't see Mr. Leigh's Jeep. The barn and parking area sat almost behind the house on the left side, so Howard crept back out of the woods, crossed the driveway, and slipped into the woods on the opposite side. He followed the edge until the barn came into view. He crouched to see it and immediately saw Mr. Leigh's Jeep parked near the back door of the house. Howard shifted and stretched for another break in the underbrush so he could see the barn. He took a few more steps and looked again. This time, Howard saw the barn, and something he hadn't expected to find parked right next to it: Ann's Jeep.

Howard didn't understand why the Jeep would be there—Mr. Leigh could have made arrangements to keep it there before he died. Maybe it had been sitting here the whole time. After a few minutes, the side door of the house swung open and Zada glided out. Howard flinched at the sight of her. Then he found what he was looking for. Behind Zada, dressed in his navy blazer and necktie, Steven Lowe emerged. Howard couldn't hear them, but they were having a conversation. Zada laughed, while Lowe closed the door behind him. They weren't in a hurry, probably going for dinner. Then Lowe pulled keys from the front pocket of his pleated khaki pants and locked the bolt on the door.

Howard, realizing they were getting ready to leave, had to move. Zada and Lowe walked down the two cement steps to the driveway and headed toward Ann's Jeep. While Lowe opened the passenger door for Zada, Howard bounded out of the weeds and ran down the driveway back to his truck. He heard the faint sound of their engine turning over and humming to life as he closed his truck door. Instead of heading back out to the road and risking getting stopped by traffic at the end of the driveway, he pulled around the fork where the driveway split between the Martins' and their neighbors. Not a minute after he got out of sight, Howard saw Lowe and Zada drive out.

In the time it took Howard to sneak back off the Martins' property, drive back through town, and arrive home, he'd worked himself into such a fuss that he almost knocked me down when he came in the back door. "Martha, I've got that son of a bitch. At least I think I do."

"Hey, watch your mouth," I nodded toward the living room, where Mary was watching cartoons. I was peeling potatoes for dinner at the sink. "And what in the world do you mean?"

Howard dropped his coat on the dining room table and was pulling his boots off. "Sorry," he glanced in at Mary and then lowered his voice. "You know how I told you about the dent in the barge? And nobody knows how it got there—not Doug or Roy or Tony?"

I nodded, setting aside a cleaned potato and picking up another.

"Well, I followed Zada all the way out to the Martin's new place south of town. Don't worry, nobody saw me. But guess what I saw."

"That's strange. The Martins aren't in town right now."

"No, they aren't, but do you know who was there? Mr. Steven Lowe." Howard watched me for a reaction, which I must have failed to deliver. "Lowe was there and so was Ann's Jeep, the same Jeep that no one's been able to find since Mr. Leigh died."

"I'm sorry, Howard, but I think I missed something. What does Lowe being in Riverside Village, driving Ann's Jeep, have to do with the barge?"

"Nothing—well, not exactly. The more I thought about it, the more I started to think that whoever took the Jeep off the island must have dented the barge. They've been doing utility work on the river, and the only thing out there I can think of that would leave a dent in that steel hull is a cement piling. Listen. Just think about the night Mr. Leigh was killed. We were all burning, all of us, even Roy, so we were distracted by the job. But not twenty-four hours earlier, Leigh found out that Zada and Ann and Lowe were all conspiring to develop the island and he sent them off. While we were burning, Zada and Lowe were supposed to be moving all their stuff from Indigo to the mainland. And they did, because all their stuff was gone the next day. But what if Lowe came back to Horne while we were all out burning?"

"Howard, what are you suggesting?"

"Listen, Martha. I don't like it any more than you do—the whole thing's been weighing on me. But Roy didn't do it. I know he didn't because when I was looking through Tony's calendars the other day, I found a note on the day Mr. Leigh died that read, 'Drop on Bariataria.' So if Tony and Roy were in on this together, which they sure seem to be, then that tells you where Roy was that night. And none of us did because we were all burning, then someone else was there. Isn't it plausible that Lowe, who was practically right next door, could have come across from Indigo, followed Leigh in Ann's Jeep, and attacked him?"

"Wait a minute—what was Roy doing?"

"Well, I don't know exactly. But I know he was on Barataria coordinating some kind of delivery. And Tony knew about it."

"I hate to ask what kind of delivery." I sat down at the dining room table while I tried to make sense of what Howard was telling me. "So why would Lowe want to attack Mr. Leigh?" I knew the answer almost as soon as I asked the question: money. Lowe stood to make a small fortune off real estate commissions, if only Leigh had agreed to let it happen.

"If Zada and Ann couldn't convince their parents to sell, then maybe Lowe thought he could get rid of Leigh on his own."

"Maybe Lowe thought he could convince him. Maybe they argued," I said. The more I thought about it, the more plausible it all seemed. And when I looked at Howard, I knew he believed it.

"And then, Lowe, in a panic, left Mr. Leigh, which accounts for the two sets of tracks at the murder scene, loaded the Jeep on the barge, and crossed the river with it, ramming the barge into the utility equipment because he didn't know what he was doing and denting it."

"So what if you're right? What now?"

"Well, the police are holding an innocent man—don't you think they'll want to know about that?"

"Yes, but you need proof, Howard. Something more than suspicion and general contempt for the man you're about to accuse of murder."

"What about the Jeep?"

"What about it? All that proves is that someone took the Jeep across the river. No one can say for sure who brought it over."

"Believe me, Martha. I didn't think much of it at first either. But think about it. The Martins haven't been to Riverside Village since right after Mr. Leigh passed away. Lowe locked the house himself, just like he lived there. And then they drove away in the Jeep—the one that no one's seen in months."

"Well, if he killed someone, why would he risk driving the missing Jeep now?"

"'Cause he thinks he's in the clear. Roy's sitting in jail. They've got their man. What's Lowe got to hide from now?"

"I don't know, Howard," and I didn't. The whole thing seemed so dark and sinister. Lowe was a creep, but was he a killer? Howard rubbed his temples. I could see him puzzling through everything in his mind. "What are you going to do?"

"Right now I'm just going to sit here and think."

"There was a story in the paper today about Horne going up for sale." I passed the *Island Packet* across the table to him. I'd folded it so the story was right on top. He picked it up and couldn't have read more than a sentence or two before he set it back down. He stood up and walked to the fridge. He pulled out a can of beer and then went out onto the porch.

March 19, 2001

⸙

THE NEXT MORNING, I RODE TO HORNE WITH HOWARD
so I could do Mrs. Leigh's hair first thing. Howard was
quiet and didn't mention our discussion from the night
before, and I didn't want to bring it up and get him
started. I figured he'd talk to me about it again when he
was ready. The Leigh's kitchen was just as quiet. Frannie
stood at the sink, rinsing the breakfast dishes and loading
them into the dishwasher. We chatted for a minute and
then fell into the solitude of our respective work. Mrs.
Leigh knew my routine, but she hadn't slept well the night
before. The overnight caregiver had trouble keeping her
in bed and said Mrs. Leigh seemed agitated or worried
about something. Mrs. Leigh fell asleep under her hood
dryer and again when I gave her a pedicure. And when
she was awake, the light in her eyes seemed dimmer than
usual. Even though I knew she couldn't answer me, I
asked her if anything was bothering her. Her Alzheimer's
came on so fast. One year she was shooting doves and
drinking mimosas and the next she couldn't be left alone.
She'd always be Mrs. Leigh, but I missed talking to her
and longed to know what she was thinking. I was slipping her stockings back on her feet when Wilma came
in to help fix lunch.

"Are you staying, Ms. Martha? Cameron and Christopher comin, and Ms. Ann say she want everyone to sit together," Wilma said.

"I'd love to stay for lunch," I said, working Mrs. Leigh's foot into her spectator. "But what's Ann up to that she wants everyone here? After the last time everyone sat down together over here, I'm not sure I can stomach it."

She shook her head. I wasn't about to leave before I found out. After the news Howard brought home the night before, I could only imagine what Ann might have to say at lunch. Just then I noticed a group of people coming up from the dock—Cameron and her husband and Christopher and his wife.

"Oh, look who's coming, Mrs. Leigh!" I said. She shifted in her seat but didn't acknowledge them beyond that. I heard them coming in through the front door and in minutes they had gathered in the kitchen around their mother. Mrs. Leigh smiled in her seat for the first time that morning.

"Good morning, mother!" Cameron sang. She was dressed in dark blue jeans and a black blazer. "We've just flown in from Los Angeles and, oh, how we've missed this view." She smiled and greeted Wilma and me. Christopher and his wife did the same.

"How's she been, Martha?" Christopher asked. He towered over us the same way Mr. Leigh had.

"Oh, she's a little quiet this morning, but no complaints otherwise," I said, watching them adjust to their surroundings and look around the way people do when they haven't been somewhere familiar in a long time. "What brings y'all to town?"

Christopher looked at his sister and then back at me. "We'll talk about that over lunch, I think. Right now I need to freshen up." He gestured towards the door and then looked at his wife, Marsha. "How about you, dear?"

"Oh," Marsha said. She was a petite woman with blond curly hair. "I feel like we've been traveling for days."

"I'm going to freshen up too," said Cameron. "Don's already headed that way and I might take a fast shower. With the time difference I feel like it's the middle of the night." She rolled her eyes breezily and they all headed back toward the guest bedrooms.

"They sold the place, you know. That's why everyone here," Wilma said to Frannie and me when everyone had gone.

I looked down at Mrs. Leigh, who was still smiling from the company, and worried Ms. Wilma was right.

"I love that we've got everyone here together like this," Zada said from her seat at the head of the table. She and Lowe arrived not long after Cameron and Christopher, and Howard hadn't taken his eyes off Lowe for one second. I can't say I was comfortable sitting at the table with him either. I kept looking at him, considering each gesture, and weighing whether or not he was capable of killing someone—of killing Mr. Andrew Leigh. Lowe had a slick exterior. He kept smiling at everyone like he belonged there and was thrilled about having lunch on Horne Island. But if Howard was right, Lowe was a potentially dangerous man, but I was too nervous about the whole thing to do anything but watch.

"I hate to think that this will be our last meal together around this table," Zada continued. She was looking at her stepsister, who didn't return Zada's smiling gaze. Zada looked at Christopher, almost as if she wanted one of them to finish saying whatever she was working herself up to say. When no one did, she continued. She looked down the table at everyone her parents employed and housed on Horne

Island, cleared her throat and said, "Oh, I'm just going to say it—the island sold. We had been so worried it would sit on the market, but just last week our agent came to us with an interested buyer. We're officially under contract. So we're celebrating today. We're celebrating."

No one spoke. Zada folded and refolded a napkin in her lap. Cameron looked down at her lunch plate. I caught Christopher's gaze, but as soon as I did, he turned his eyes to his lap. Zada beamed obliviously. And Ann looked like a deer caught in headlights. Wilma was also looking at her lap, shaking her head back and forth as if she'd heard something unbelievable. Doug put his arm around his wife. Toot shook his head. Howard looked at me with his eyebrows raised, then returned to staring at Lowe, who must have sensed the tension that gripped the table because he broke the silence.

"Now I know you all probably heard about the development plans Zada and I had been working on, and I honestly thought our plans would please everyone at this table. I was wrong about that, and since getting to know everyone and spending time around town, I've realized that maybe Mr. Leigh was right about keeping this place. And if you'd have asked me a year ago if I wanted to go hunting on some secluded island, I'd have said no way." Lowe chuckled and shifted in his seat. He looked at Zada, who was smiling expectantly at him, and then kept talking. "I want you all to know that this buyer understands what you've all built here and they want to maintain the character of this place just like you do. So even though I pushed for it before, I am happy to say the new owners don't plan to develop."

"See," Zada said. "We're celebrating."

"Losin' our jobs don't seem like somethin' to celebrate," Wilma muttered. Everyone looked at her when she spoke—

the first of any of us to say anything against them—which seemed to give her strength. "I just can't believe what y'all are doin' to destroy what your parents built. Everything they done, every promise they made, you just come and pull apart. And it start with sendin' my boy to jail for somethin' y'all probably did yourselves. Shame on all of you—especially you, Cameron, for lettin' those two do it."

Ann flinched in her seat. Cameron looked like she might cry. But Zada weathered the attack with a flush of exasperation.

"Well, Zada, while we're making announcements, why don't you tell everyone the reason we're selling the island," Christopher said, straightening up in his chair.

"Now, I don't think that's anyone's business." Zada twitched nervously and adjusted her shawl like it was armor.

"Oh, for goodness sakes," Cameron said. "They'll find out anyway, Zada. They need to hear it from us." She turned and looked at everyone around the table. "Wilma, everyone, Zada and Ann hired a lawyer to sue us for the expenses of keeping up the island. We have to sell it because they want their money. That's why you're losing your jobs, Wilma and Doug and Toot." She rose from her chair. "Now, if you'll excuse me. I don't much feel like eating anymore."

None of us knew it at the time, but even after Mr. Leigh put a stop to Zada, Ann, and Lowe's development plans, the sisters kept pushing their step-brother and step-sister about selling the island. Mr. Leigh's death only strengthened their argument. Ann and Zada just couldn't stand spending their money on Horne and refused to recognize its nostalgic and familial value, so in the end, they hired attorneys and sued Cameron and Christopher for back-expenses and half the cost of running the place every year the family owned the property.

Cameron and Christopher didn't live in Riverside Village, but they spent time there with their parents every year and it was special to them. They made memories in those dove fields and along those trails. Cameron once told me that she loved the island because it reminded her of her parents in their youth. When she came to Horne Island, she could see her mother tending the camellias in her sunhat and her father riding his horse in his tattered field jacket like ghosts of a happier time. But in the end, they didn't have had the money to repay Zada and Ann.

"Really, the arrangement couldn't have been better. We don't have much time to get the main house cleared out. But the new owner is giving everyone an extra six weeks to get settled elsewhere," Zada's smile had faded, but the sing-songy hopefulness of her voice didn't waver. "And they'll let us bury mother next to dad, when the time comes, which Ann and I couldn't be happier about. Right, Ann?"

She looked at Ann, and Ann fidgeted with her napkin. A bead of sweat dripped down Ann's forehead when she nodded.

"And we're going to need everyone's help to get mother situated on the mainland. I wanted to take her back to New York with me, but the Martins have offered to let her stay at their place in town. Mother loved that house, and Wilma and Frannie, we'd like to keep you on over there. You'll have to find a place to live, but we'll work out the particulars and keep you on as long as you want to stay. Dad and Mother would have wanted it that way."

Then, out of nowhere, Ann stood up so fast she bumped the table. "If you'll excuse me," she said as she rushed out of the room with such urgency I wondered if she might be sick.

"Is she okay?" Sue whispered to Doug.

"Well," Zada continued as if she didn't notice. "We can work out the details later this afternoon. You've all got a lot to absorb, I understand that." She placed her napkin next to her plate and got up to leave. Lowe followed her out the front, leaving Howard, Wilma, Doug, Sue, Frannie, Toot, and me still sitting around stunned.

"She act like she's doin' somebody a favor," Wilma said. "Now where am I goin' to go. Been here all my life and ain't never wanted to leave. Now what?" She stacked a plate of dishes and carried them into the kitchen.

"I'll help you clean up," I said, standing and collecting a stack of plates.

APRIL 7, 2001

WILMA AND I MET ON SATURDAY MORNING TO GO through all the Leighs' clothing and personal things, packing what Mrs. Leigh needed and donating the rest. Under the deadline of the real estate closing, everyone focused on shutting down Horne Island operations and moving Mrs. Leigh to the mainland. All the children boxed up what they wanted from the house—old paintings, Mrs. Leigh's Blue Willow china—and shipped it to their respective homes across the country. Cameron and Christopher left town after a few days so they could get back to work. Zada and Ann, by this time, had set up camp on Horne, though no one saw much of them during those weeks because they were busy planning an oyster roast to celebrate the move. Walls and spaces emptied piece by piece. Seeing everything being dismantled felt so strange. Tony helped Howard sell what was left of the horses. Most of the housewares and furnishings were donated—Doug and Toot took boxes by the boatload to the church thrift store. Frannie packed up and moved everything she needed to run the kitchen at the Martins' house in town.

"I think we can keep some of this on hangers, if we bag it up, which will make unpacking it easier," I said, surveying the job.

"Mmm hmm," Wilma agreed from outside the closet door. She pulled open the top drawer of the antique dresser, removed a neat stack of underclothes, and placed them into a cardboard box on the bed. The caregiver had Mrs. Leigh set up in the kitchen, getting her ready for the trip across the river. Mrs. Leigh was used to going back and forth for doctors appointments and I liked to think that crossing the river still thrilled her the way it always had before she got sick. But I knew she liked the trip to Horne better than she liked the trip from. We'd all been talking to her about the move, whether or not she understood. The girls went though their mother's closet and took what they wanted of her fancier things. She didn't have much by that point, but Mrs. Leigh had a few evening gowns and formal suiting leftover from her New York life. By the time Wilma and I got in their to pack up Mrs. Leigh's clothes, only her everyday wardrobe—the navy pants and crisp dress shirts—remained in her tidy wall closet.

The Leigh's bedroom was as plain and understated as the rest of the house. The furnishings were sturdy and unadorned, and a plain quilt covered the bed. I wrapped a stack of shirts from the closet in a plastic bag and laid them into a box. The afternoon sun was shining in through the wall of windows, but the air in the room felt heavy and thick. Ever since Howard told me about his suspicions, I'd had a nervous feeling in my stomach. And I didn't know if I should tell Wilma or not. I didn't want to get her hopes up that Roy would be set free, but I also wondered if she knew anything that might help. Plus, seeing the boxes reminded me of moving PJ just months before. So much had changed in such a short span of time, I felt dizzy.

"Ms. Wilma, do you mind if I crack open a window? I'm feeling a little overwhelmed."

"I know the feelin'," she laughed and kept on emptying the dresser.

I unlatched the window closest to the bed and pushed it open. It wasn't much cooler outside, but a breeze was blowing in off the water, bringing with it the scent of the ocean. "Have you heard anything from Roy's lawyer?"

"Nothin' that gives me any hope," she said, closing an empty dresser drawer and opening the next one down. "They keep sayin' the evidence is shaky, but they don't have no better ideas."

She didn't offer any more, so I didn't press her. "Well, I'm sure when he gets out, Roy will be surprised by all the changes around here. I know I can barely keep up we're closing the place down so fast. Howard said he's going to finish clearing out the barn today. The changes are almost too much to bear."

"Change gon' come, Ms. Martha. Best you can do is keep goin'. I just never thought I'd see it come about like this on Horne Island." She lowered a stack of Mrs. Leigh's nightclothes into the now-full box, patting them carefully into place and folding the box lid closed. Then she looked around the room and wrung her hands. "Do you have the marker? I want to label this box 'fore it ends up lost in the shuffle."

I passed it to her and patted her on the arm. "I know this must be difficult for you—more difficult than anyone else probably."

Wilma marked the box in her shaky hand, "Mrs. Leigh's dresser," and passed back the marker. She smiled at me, and then looked out the window at the river. "The first time I come here was with my daddy. Back then the Beaches still owned Horne, wasn't even a decent house here, and Mr. Leigh's dad owned Honey Horn plantation on Hilton Head. I remember thinkin' Horne Island was the biggest wilderness I ever set foot in. The Beaches farmed it, but most everything was woods. I never thought Horne Island could be any more than a farm in the middle of nowhere. Then the Crosley's bought it, built the house and everything, but I'd never seen it before. All I knew of this place was forest and the old slave cemetery, which gave me a fright as a child. I had nightmares about what might lurk on Horne Island." She closed the drawer she'd just emptied and pulled open the last one in the dresser. "Then I grew up and Mr. Leigh bought the island off the Crosley's and put me in charge of the house. I remember movin' out here when Roy was still young. Packin' my boxes and bringin' them over on the boat, worryin' I was going back to the wild forest. I remember seein' this house for the first time and thinkin', my goodness, how a place can change. Now, here I am, packin' up my boxes and headin' back the other way. Least I still get to be with Mrs. Leigh. If they'd say they was takin' her up to New York or California, I wouldn't even have a job."

"I remember when they were building this house, now that you mention it. I used to sit and watch the barge, filled with lumber and construction materials, crossin' the river. I thought they must be building the biggest house in the world, the amount of stuff they brought over. And I remember when Mr. Leigh bought the place. Horne Island really hasn't been the same since he passed."

"Not only is Mr. Leigh gone, but they got my son in jail for killin' him. Roy don't even get to say goodbye to the place for we got to find some place to go."

Just then, I heard Howard yell for me from the front of the house. "I'm back here, in Mrs. Leigh's room," I yelled.

A moment later he was standing in the doorway. "The medical transport is here."

"We're about done," I said.

"How are you, Ms. Wilma? Handling this move okay?"

"Oh, Mr. Howard, thank you, sir, for askin'. To tell you the truth, ain't nothin' more awful than packin' up this house and knowin' it gon be the last time. Ms. Martha and I were just talkin' about it."

"Today was not easy, Ms. Wilma. Going through all the old stuff out in the barn and Tony's office—everything seems to have memories attached to it."

"You're tellin' me, Mr. Howard. You're tellin' me." She surveyed the room, now emptied and boxed up. "Are y'all ready to take her over?"

"We can leave whenever you're ready."

"We should go before she gets too tired," I said.

We'd timed Mrs. Leigh's departure with the high tide, so the pitch on the dock wouldn't be so steep. The homecare agency sent two sturdy young men to help ferry her across. The taller one pushed her wheelchair out of the house and down to the dock. When Mrs. Leigh was beside the boat, the tall guy climbed down into the boat and the other took the handles on her chair. They lifted her, chair and all, down in. Then Doug, Howard, Wilma, the caregiver, and I boarded and sat. We locked Mrs. Leigh's chair next to Howard, who drove, so she could see where we were headed. The high afternoon sun sparkled on the water. The air felt warm, already thickening with summertime humidity. Cottony white clouds marched across the azure sky. As Howard pulled up to the mainland dock, Mrs. Leigh stiffened and smiled in her seat. I hated to think that this might be her last ride across the river she loved so much. I wanted so much to feel good about this inevitable trip, to be able to appreciate Mrs. Leigh's final days. But Wilma was right; Mr. Leigh's absence cast a gloomy shadow even on such a beautiful afternoon.

I held Mrs. Leigh's elbow as she shuffled off the dock and across the parking lot. Doug, Wilma, and the caregiver took her to the Martins', where Wilma wanted her settled before dinner. Frannie was already there cooking Mrs. Leigh's favorite duck in wine sauce for dinner.

"Let me know if you need any help once you get there," I said to Wilma as she got in the car. She nodded as Doug pulled away, leaving Howard and me standing in the gravel parking lot.

Howard put his arm around me as we walked to his truck. "You know, Martha, I didn't want to say this in front of Wilma earlier, but the hardest thing for me about moving the Leigh's off Horne for good was swallowing the truth."

"What do you mean?"

"Well, all these years, I've been spending time over there, working and helping out, and having the time of my life in those woods. I called everyone on that island my friend. And never once did I suspect anyone of being anything other than honest and straightforward. But now I've come to find out that everything wasn't always as it seemed."

April 27, 2001

DOUG WAS DUMPING A BASKET OF STEAMY OYSTERS onto one of the four shucking tables that lined the back of the Martins' yard when Howard and I arrived at Zada's party. Then, in seconds, hungry guests surrounded the pile of shellfish. It seemed like everyone in town had come to eat. People mingled in small groups around the yard, but the only person I searched the crowd for was Steven Lowe. Howard hadn't said so, but I could tell he was looking for Lowe too. The only reason he'd agreed to come was because I told him Lowe would probably be here—I assumed he would anyways. Roy had been in jail for over a month, refusing to let his mother use her entire savings to bail him out. Each day, Howard seemed to grow more agitated. He had gone through every piece of paper from Tony's office countless times, looking for some piece of evidence, any piece of evidence, but he didn't know what. Lowe had coordinated the real estate development plans and the DNR bust, and Howard was convinced he had something to do with Mr. Leigh's murder. Howard wanted to talk to Lowe and had gone by the Martins' place at least twice looking for him, but Lowe hadn't been around since they announced the island had sold. He seemed to have disappeared.

"Get them while they're hot," Zada said when she saw Howard and me. "Isn't this wonderful?"

I smiled, but didn't feel much like celebrating. Aside from my nerves about Howard and Lowe, Mother said she saw someone else's boat coming and going from the Horne Island mainland house, and this information felt so sad. I couldn't just jump on the boat and ride over there myself. I couldn't let myself into the mainland house without committing trespass. Horne Island didn't belong to us anymore, and I just couldn't seem to feel festive about that at all.

"Isn't it a little late in the year for oysters?" Howard said to Zada. Mr. Lowe was surprisingly not by her side.

"April has an R," Zada said with slight affront.

"I suppose it does."

"Yes, well, make yourselves comfortable. Everyone is here. Mom is up on the porch. And, Mr. Howard, make sure you get plenty of oysters. This is your last chance," Zada bubbled. "Now, if you'll pardon me, I believe I just saw the Miller's and I want to say hello."

"I'm going to say hello to Mrs. Leigh," I said to Howard after Zada floated on.

"I'm going to see if I can't find Mr. Lowe."

"Howard, what are you going to do?"

"I just want to have a talk with the man." He held up his hands in innocence.

"I don't believe that, but I'm going to leave you to it and go see Mrs. Leigh. Don't do anything foolish." I smiled at him and then walked across the lawn to the house.

Wilma had Mrs. Leigh set up on the back porch in her wheelchair. She seemed to have wilted there. Her clothes looked crisp and proper as always, but inside them, her body looked more shrunken and frail. Her head was resting on the cushion and her eyes looked down, rather than at the party surrounding her.

"She's tired today," Wilma said, standing next to her.

"Well, she's had a long week," I squeezed Mrs. Leigh's hand and knelt beside her, but her gaze didn't lift. "How are you holding up, Ms. Wilma?"

"Oh, I fine," she said. "The evening caregiver is runnin' late today, so I'm here for the party even though this the last place I want to be."

Wilma was still living in her cottage on Horne, but she was only allowed to stay on for another few weeks before she had to move off for good. She still hadn't found a place. She'd been so busy moving Mrs. Leigh that she probably hadn't had time to look.

"Now, you just let me know when you're ready to start looking for a place over here," I said, "and we'll do everything we can to help you find a good place."

"I know, Ms. Martha, I know it's time to find somethin'."

Mrs. Leigh looked like she might fall asleep in her chair. When her head started slipping sideways, Wilma said, "We better get Mrs. Leigh inside. She can't wait for my help to arrive, so would you mind?"

"Not at all," I stood to help Wilma move Mrs. Leigh's wheelchair. She had a dazed look when her eyes opened and saw us, but she woke up when we started wheeling her. With Wilma pushing and me following, we walked Mrs. Leigh into the back door and into the Martin's kitchen. We were only halfway through the small eat-in when Ann came in through the butler's pantry where we were headed.

"Oh, are you taking Mom to bed already?" she said when she saw us. Her eyes darted anxiously around the room as she spoke. Her social awkwardness was most pronounced when you bumped into her like that, like she had been caught off-guard and didn't know what to say. She'd always been awkward.

"She startin' to drift," Wilma said. Then a confused look came over her face. "Ms. Ann, this might seem strange, but you wearin' Roy's jacket?"

"What?" Ann acted as if Wilma were speaking a different language.

"Your jacket—it Roy's. I tried to find it when they packed up the barn and couldn't find it anywhere."

"Oh, this jacket?" Ann looked down at the brown, faded garment. "It could be. I just picked it up off the barn rack one night and have been wearing it ever since."

"Well, can I have it?"

Ann laughed nervously and hesitated before removing the jacket, handing it to Wilma, and saying good night to her mother. Then she scurried out the door.

"That was strange," I said to Wilma after she'd gone.

"That woman always strange," Wilma said with a dry laugh. We continued to Mrs. Leigh's room, where we'd just parked her next to the bed when the caregiver came in.

"I'm so sorry I'm late," Debbie—one of the two women who helped Mrs. Leigh—said. She was a young, energetic woman with her curly hair tied back in a high ponytail. "My car wouldn't start—again! How is she tonight?"

"She tired, so we fixin' her for bed."

"Well, why don't you ladies get back to the party. I can take it from here."

"If you don't think you gonna need me, then I'm headin' home for the night," Wilma said. She and I both said good night to Mrs. Leigh and left Debbie to get her ready.

"I suppose I'm ready to start lookin' at places as soon as you find somethin' to show me," Wilma said as she gathered her things from the kitchen.

"Okay, then, Ms. Wilma. I'm happy to help." I patted her on the shoulder as she left through the front of the house. I watched her go, then poured myself a glass of white zin from the bottle in the refrigerator and walked back out onto the porch.

In the light from the fire in the corner of the yard, I saw Howard standing next to Doug, who was still manning the steam pit. The crowd seemed to have grown. A group of teenagers—most of whom I recognized because of their parents—gathered on the grass by the river. All four shucking tables had people working around them. I recognized several of my neighbors and acquaintances in the crowd. I didn't see Steven Lowe and hoped that didn't mean Howard had run him off.

"I didn't think Zada knew this many people in town," I said when I walked up to Howard and Doug. The fire felt hot and unpleasant on the warm night. "Can you take a break to eat?"

"I was just thinking the same thing," Howard said. "Doug, I'll come find you later."

Howard and I walked around the parameter of the crowd. "So any sign of Lowe?" I asked when we'd found a spot at a table piled with a steaming batch of oysters.

"Not one," he said.

"Well, it is strange that he's not here, isn't it?"

"Maybe he took his money and ran." We smiled and nodded to the people next to us and were lost in small talk before I could ask Howard any more.

To Zada's credit, the spread looked wonderful. Oyster

knives and towels were stacked at one side of each table, and the opposite sides had bowls of butter and hot sauce and crackers. My whole life, I've heard people say the Chrystal River oysters are the best on the earth. People in Riverside Village may just be partial to our own, but I've never had an oyster that compared. They weren't chewy or slimy—just salty and slippery and good. I cracked open one after the other on a big cluster of eight, scooping each shellfish from its mud-crusted shell. They were delicious. Howard worked in silence next me, popping open shells and eating.

Just then, Betsy Sims from church and her sister came up beside me. "Hello, Martha. Howard," she smiled. "Aren't these oysters beautiful? I'll miss eating like this all summer."

"They are good too," Howard nodded at her.

"So how did Mrs. Leigh do on the move across the river?" she asked me.

"Oh, she's all right," I said. "She was sitting outside for a while tonight. You just missed her."

"Well, I've been thinking about her. Such a terrible thing about Mr. Leigh."

I nodded, but didn't take her bait, if indeed she was fishing for gossip. I just kept my mouth shut about Mr. Leigh and changed the subject. "So, Betsy, will you be working the church booth at Mayfest this year?"

"Oh, you know I will, Martha," Betsy said, leaving the topic of the Leigh's behind. "I don't think they could do it without me."

"You're probably right," I beamed at her. She was telling me about some problem or another with organizing the booth when Howard interrupted us.

"I hate to eat and run, ladies, but I have an early day tomorrow."

He was lying, but I played along, shrugging at Betsy. "He's my ride home, but I'll see you in a few weeks."

Howard led me around to the side of the house by a big live oak. The sun had begun to set, making everything under the tree look shadowy and dark. It turned out Lowe had been called back to New York for a real estate closing or something like that. So whatever business Howard had with him, had to wait. As I got in the passenger side of Howard's truck, I thought again about how strange it was that Ann was wearing Roy's jacket.

May 12, 2001

⎯⎯⎯⎯⎯

THE LAST TIME I SAW MRS. LEIGH ALIVE WAS THE DAY of the Riverside Village Village Festival—Mayfest, as we called it around town, always happened on the same weekend as Mother's Day. That particular year, the festival was special because the Riverside Village Historical Preservation Society recently purchased the Heyward House on the corner of Boundary and Bridge Streets. The house, previously owned by the Heyward family, had been built in the early 1840s and was one of the few places that wasn't burned down in the Civil War. They'd fixed up the inside of the house to make it into a museum and were holding a gala to show off what they had done. The town blocked off the end of Calhoun Street closest to the water and a good crowd had gathered by the time my mother and I arrived. People mingled in the street, enjoying what was left of the cool spring weather. The line for the Church of the Cross's shrimp salad sandwiches, which everyone loved, snaked around the table. Across the street booths were set up in the Methodist Church yard. The sun blazed high and warm in the blue sky. The breeze blew heavy enough to keep the gnats away but not heavy enough to be bothersome.

Despite the festive atmosphere, an anxious feeling gripped me. I'd heard from Wilma that Lowe had returned to Riverside Village two days before, and I knew Howard would be looking for him. I tried to distract myself by enjoying the day.

As part of the special events, the Hallelujah Singers had been invited to perform at the Church of the Cross. This was a big deal because they'd recently been in *Forrest Gump* and Mother and I were looking forward to seeing them live. The street fair wrapped up by mid-afternoon and we started making our way toward the river and the church. Inside, the wooden pews were filling with people, fidgeting and getting themselves settled, talking to neighbors and friends. Mother and I found end seats near the back and not long after we did, the singers walked onstage in a single file line. The stir in the church settled in anticipation. They were dressed in colorful clothing and even in the back where we were sitting I could see the singers smiling. For a few minutes everyone was quiet. But when they started singing, the whole crowd started moving and singing along. The place was just full of joy and song, and Mother said she was thrilled history and culture were being preserved through their performance. I knew Mrs. Leigh would have loved it too.

When we came out of the Church of the Cross, I said to Mother, "Let's go back and visit Mrs. Leigh." The house that she'd been staying in since everything happened on Horne Island was right behind the church.

Mother and I walked around the side of the church and up to the house. I knocked and then let us in, calling out, "Hello, anybody home?"

"Hello, Ms. Martha," Mrs. Wilma called from the kitchen. "And hello, Ms. Martha," she said as she came out to greet us. "How are you?"

"We're fine," I said, "we've just come from the May Fest and wanted to stop by to check on Mrs. Leigh."

"That's fine." Wilma nodded. Her eyes were bright but tired.

"How's Roy holding up?" I asked her quietly.

Ms. Wilma hung her head for a moment. "They good thing about him sitting in jail is I know he ain't getting into more trouble with Barbara. I don't suppose you brought me a Hersey bar?" she changed the subject from her son's troubles.

"You know, I didn't," I laughed, knowing she was teasing me.

I could smell Frannie's buttermilk cornbread baking in the oven. "Will you ladies be staying for dinner?" she asked us.

"No, thank you, Frannie. We're just dropping in on Mrs. Leigh," I said. "How is she today?"

"Well, you can go on back and see her," said Ms. Wilma.

I found Mrs. Leigh sitting in one of the bedrooms. They had her set up in a wooden chair near the window. The Chrystal River glistened with the oncoming sunset. She couldn't see Horne Island from there, but she could see Palmetto Bluff, which was so wooded and green it almost looked the same. I like to think Mrs. Leigh, through the fog of her Alzheimer's, saw her beloved island despite geography.

I knelt down in front of her and asked how she was doing. I knew by the way she shifted in her seat that she knew I was there and recognized me. She seemed to know people by the tone of their voice and she may have thought I was there to work on her and was sitting up to get ready. Mrs. Leigh's hair was as perfect as it was when I met her, just the way she liked it.

"Oh, Mrs. Leigh, I've been at the festival all day and I've been to see the Hallelujah Singers," I said. She smiled when I mentioned the festival.

I was still doing Mrs. Leigh's hair once a week, but I came by as often as I could. If I'd learned anything over the past several months, it was not to take anyone for granted. After about thirty minutes, I heard voices in the front room and thought it was the visiting nurse. In addition to Frannie cooking and Ms. Wilma keeping house, Ms. Leigh still had caregivers, and a nurse came in to check on her several times a week.

"Well, Mrs. Leigh," I said as I stood up to leave. "Mother and I are off. I'm meeting Howard at the big party at the Heyward House."

As soon as I mentioned the party, Mrs. Leigh perked up in her chair and smiled. Mrs. Leigh loved a party. I smiled at how excited she looked, like she needed to get ready to go. But after a few moments, that familiar light was gone and she slumped back down again. Her gaze seemed more distant than ever as we left her in her room.

Mother and I greeted the caregiver and said our good-byes to Frannie and Ms. Wilma as we walked through the house and toward the door. Just before walking out, I touched Ms. Wilma on the arm and said, "Keep a close eye on her tonight."

Mrs. Wilma covered my hand with hers and nodded as I slipped out the door behind Mother.

Mother and I went home to freshen up and pick up Howard before driving back downtown for the gala. When we pulled up, carts lined the street and people were overflowing from the yard. Everyone in town had come. We greeted the Jones on the walk up and passed a group of teenagers mingling by the fence. The Heyward House glowed in the fading light. Live oaks as old as the house cloaked it in moss covered branches. The house, a two-story white Carolina-style farmhouse with black shutters, was built in the 1840s. Aside from fresh coats of paint, not much about the outside had changed over the years. The Heywards owned it for over a hundred years before selling it to the Historical Society. Even the summer kitchen and slave quarters still stood in the back.

White tents were arranged with a buffet of barbeque and red rice underneath. Reeves had catered, and I saw the Nelsons and Millers in the food line. The Millers had only been back in town for a few days. Everyone had donned their "Riverside Village attire," per the invitations—flip flops and pearls on the women and shorts, dress shirts, and bow ties for the men. All the tables were dressed in white tablecloths with centerpieces of magnolia flowers, greenery, and candles. On the opposite side of the yard, a band was playing music and people were dancing. Up on the porch, tables of deserts were set up and crowded with people filling plates.

As soon as she saw Mother, Hattie Leonard, the president of the Historical Society, approached us and said hello.

"Isn't this wonderful," Mother said.

"Oh, thank you, we worked very hard to get everything pulled together," Hattie said. "There was a last-minute emergency with the desserts, but everything worked out. I'm so relieved."

"Well, you've drawn a crowd," I said. "Everyone in town is here."

"I tell you what, I'm just glad it's finally here. You can't imagine the work that went into this evening." She glanced around the yard, admiring her work. "Say, Howard, did you see they broke ground on the new development?"

"I did see that," Howard said. "And I also saw the Harpers are looking to sell their piece of property along the new parkway."

"I know. I can't believe it."

"I suppose they want to strike while the iron is hot," Howard said, " and get as much money out of the place as they can."

"That's just the way it is, I suppose." We chatted a few more minutes then Hattie took Mother inside to show her everything they'd done to remodel the inside. "Make sure you get some of that barbeque," she called to Howard and me as they walked away. "It's so tender you don't even have to chew it."

Howard and I headed for the food line. The subject of real estate development reminded me of the Leighs. Mrs. Leigh would have loved to come to the party. When they came to town, they liked to get involved. Mrs. Leigh participated in the Historical Society and the Garden Club, and they went to the Church of the Cross. Everybody knew them. And purchasing the house was a big deal for the Historical Society. It was one of the few buildings in town that wasn't burned in the war, and it hadn't been changed much since then either.

"I went to see Mrs. Leigh this afternoon and I'm probably going to be very thankful that I went," I told Howard as we filled our plates. I had a feeling she was slipping away and I wanted to tell Howard about it. Then, as I turned to look for a table, I noticed Zada across the yard, laughing and waving her shawl dramatically. My stomach sank when I saw Lowe's coiffed blond head just behind her. Howard saw him as soon as he turned around. "Well, look who's back in town."

In that moment, he seemed to forget about the plate full of barbeque and slaw in his hand. He didn't take his eyes off Lowe until we'd made our way to an empty table near the center of the crowd. "Martha," he said earnestly. "If you'll excuse me for a minute. I don't think I can eat before I have a word with Mr. Lowe."

I looked down at my plate of food and back at Howard. "Well, I'm coming with you then."

Abandoning our food and table, we crossed the crowd of people to where Zada and Lowe were now standing alone.

"Martha and Howard," Zada fluttered when she saw us approaching. "How are you?"

"Zada," Howard acknowledged her and then looked at Lowe. "A word, Lowe?"

"Sure, Howard," Lowe said with a nervous laugh. "What can I help you with?"

"Funny thing," Howard looked around to see who was in earshot. "I ran into Calvin Espy the other day.

Lowe looked confused.

"You know, from the DNR."

"Oh, yes, Espy." Lowe nodded and shrugged. "How could I forget?"

"Yeah, how could you forget? He was the guy who wrote us all tickets last winter. Anyways, I ran into him and he got to talking about that very same day."

"And how is Calvin these days?" Lowe squirmed.

"You know what he said? He said you actually had something to do with us all getting in trouble."

Lowe's eyes widened and he looked at Zada. "Now Howard, Steven got a ticket too, you remember," she said.

"I do remember that, Zada. But come to think of it, maybe you were in on it too."

"Oh, Howard, what does that matter? It was so long ago. Dad's dead. The island has been sold. It's over," Zada said.

"You're right, the island's gone," Howard said. "But Roy's still in jail. For a crime he didn't commit. And so I don't think it's over."

Zada looked confused.

But something flashed across Lowe's face—a realization, maybe, or knowing. "Howard, what does that have to do with the DNR?" he said, running his fingers through his hair.

"I don't know, Lowe. I mean, it seems to me that someone who could conspire to sell an island out from under a man and would intentionally get that same man in trouble with the law—and try to hide it on top of that by getting a ticket too—would be the first person I'd want to talk to about that man's murder."

"Howard Smith," Zada started to shriek but caught herself and looked around to make sure no one heard her. A few couples that were standing near us raised their eyebrows and glanced in our direction, but they went right back to their conversation and no one seemed to notice. "That's a terrible thing to say. And if you want to know the truth, I put him up to the thing with the DNR. I wanted Dad to get in trouble so he'd have to sell the island. That's all. It was my idea. Steven just went along with it. And he was on Indigo that night."

Lowe's gloss seemed to be melting. He shifted his weight from foot to foot and looked at Zada.

"Do you know that for sure, Zada? You were with him the whole night." I asked her.

She looked at me and back at Steven. "Well, almost. He went back to pick up a load, but we told the police all this. Roy is sitting in jail for a reason. Now, if you'll excuse us, I've had enough of this talk."

156   *Martha C.*

"Lowe?" Howard said, taking a step forward and puffing out his chest a little. He needed to hear it from him.

Lowe's face twitched with a pained expression, and he looked at Zada. "I don't know what happened that night."

"I told you," Zada spat at us. She linked her arm in Lowe's and pulled him into the crowd.

When they'd gone, I asked Howard if he believed him.

"No, I don't suppose I do."

Howard and I didn't stay at the party. We left then and dropped Mother at home and went home ourselves. During the night, when the caregiver came to check Mrs. Leigh, she found Mrs. Leigh had passed away. Mrs. Wilma called me the next morning to let me know.

May 15, 2001

<hr/>

Now here we are, paying our respects to Mrs. Leigh without any further sense of what happened to Mr. Leigh. When I told mother what happened with Howard and Steven Lowe, she asked if I believed Lowe. I suppose I want to, and I have, I admit, considered that maybe the police arrested the right man. But for all Roy's flaws, he would have to utter the words himself before I could believe he killed Mr. Leigh, and I'm not even sure I would then. I'm pondering how to come to terms with the possibility of never knowing what happened that night, when organ music fills the church, signaling the close of Mrs. Leigh's funeral service.

I stand and help mother to the aisle, joining the trickling stream of the Leigh's children and friends. We all walk quietly outside, where a gust of wind hits us and thunder grumbles in the distance.

"My goodness," says Mother, clutching the hem of her skirt. The sky is still dark and churning, but it's not raining, at least not yet.

"We could all blow away out here," I say, firming up my hold on her arm. PJ makes her way to us through the dispersing crowd. The weather quickens the condolences or courtesies that would have normally taken place on the church stairs and most of the guests filter to their cars and head for home.

"I'm certain I don't feel up to a boat ride," Mother says.

"That's okay; I don't either. I'll take you home," PJ offers, holding her jacket closed against the wind. She is probably happy to get the pass from seeing Tony on Horne Island.

"You're sure?" I ask.

"Yes, I'm sure."

"Well, my dear, give my condolences again to the family," Mother says as we prepare to part ways. "They haven't had an easy year. None of you have."

"Of course," I say. Then, tearing up a little, "I just wish there could be more peace."

Mother pats my shoulder and gives me a moment to collect myself. "Time tells all and heals all."

I smile weakly at her and hug PJ one more time before they go and I make my way to the boat. The small group left, those of us closest to Mrs. Leigh—her children and their families, Wilma, Frannie, PJ, and Sue—gather on the dock, where Doug has the Horne Island boat ready to take us all across. The Martins and another couple from the Leighs' church follow in their boats. The trip is quiet, everyone seeming to be in his or her own little world. Mrs. Leigh's remains sit in the cabin next to Christopher. The wind still comes in gusts, but Tony is waiting when we arrive on Horne with wagons and Jeeps.

"Where's PJ?" he asks me when everyone is loading up.

"She didn't come. She actually took my mother home after the service."

He hangs his head with disappointment for a second and then says, "I was saving a seat for her on the wagon."

I nod but don't respond. As much as I love those two together, I knew he didn't have a chance. And I feel sorry for him. We ride in a caravan to the place on the top end of the island where Mr. Leigh is buried. Tony has the hole ready to go—she was cremated, so the burying task is easier than it could have been. Putting Mrs. Leigh in the ground next to Mr. Leigh feels right and unfair at the same time. Losing them both in such a short time is hardest, I think, as Christopher says a prayer and throws a ceremonial handful of dirt in the grave. While everyone mingles around the burial sight, I walk down closer to the river and look out across the sound. The water is dark gray with white crests. Beyond the water sits Hilton Head Island, a place that was, at one time, not so different from Horne. Now it's a popular tourist destination with millions of visitors flooding the place every summer. Although today I feel like I'm looking into a different world, I can't help wondering if I'm also looking at the future. Even from across the sound I can feel the presence of change and development closing in on Riverside Village.

"We better get back 'fore the weather gets worse," Wilma says coming up beside me.

I ride on the wagon with Wilma, Zada, Lowe, and Cameron and Christopher and their families, as we take the Evening Trail for what I'm sure will be my last time. I try to take it all in, the gray clouds passing over brilliant green trees, the damp piney smell of the forest, and then notice Lowe gazing almost as lovingly as I am at the scenery. He nudges Zada, who's seated next to him. "Such a shame to leave this place for good, isn't it?"

Wilma raises an eyebrow at him but doesn't speak.

"Ugh, good riddance," Zada says.

When we arrive back at the dock, I look at the house. It feels so strange to be here again, visiting the place like a tourist allowed one last look before the attraction closes forever. Then I step into the boat and sit between Lowe and Wilma. The tide has nearly gone all the way out and the muddy creek bottom edges are exposed and crawling with fiddler grabs. The overcast sky no longer threatens imminent rain, but the water is choppy when we exit the creek and the wind still whipping. Doug slowly follows behind the Martins' boat, dipping and bucking on the water, waves smacking the hull and splashing over all of us the whole time. After pressing myself into my seat the whole ride, I am so grateful when the dock by the church comes into view. But there are people gathered.

"Who is that on the dock?" I ask no one in particular. I soon recognize Howard and two police officers. Then a fourth person steps out from behind Howard. "Is that Roy?"

Wilma nearly jumps off the boat to get a better view. "It is him!" she shrieks. "He ain't wearin' no jail uniform either."

Everyone is standing now, barely able in the rocking boat, to see that Roy, after all these months, is standing free on the dock. Knowing Howard is behind this, I look at Lowe, who almost looks as confused as the rest of us. But then I realize he's not looking at the dock; he's looking at Ann.

Ann lifts her leg onto the gunwale. She turns to Lowe, who is still watching her, and says, "I can't do this anymore," and, like a dancer launching herself into the air, she jumps overboard and lands in the violent water.

Shock and chaos ensue, as Doug stops the boat and we all frantically search the surface of the water for her.

"Did she fall?" Doug asks.

"I think she jumped," Wilma says with wide eyes. The waves toss us and I lose sight of where Ann had been. Zada nearly hyperventilating, screams for someone to save her sister.

"I'm trying, Ms. Zada," Doug says, "but I can't save her if I can't find her."

The police onshore seem to realize we're in trouble. One of the officers runs down the dock to their car and the other paces the end of the dock with his radio in his hand. I search the water. I'm not sure what to think, and then I notice Lowe in more agony than Zada. "Mr. Lowe," I say confused. "Are you all right?"

"All I wanted to do was talk to him," Lowe says through heavy, panicked breaths. He's slouched on the boat bench, rocking back and forth. "I just wanted to take him for a ride and show him my vision. But then he was so mad about the DNR thing and it all went wrong."

A stunned silence falls over the boat. Mr. Lowe's ramblings trail off when he realizes everyone is watching him. Thinking he's about to confess, I say, "I think you better start from the beginning."

Mr. Lowe takes a deep breath to pull himself together and then explains what happened the night of Mr. Leigh's death. He'd been on Indigo that night with Zada, packing his things, when they got into an argument. Zada refused to go back to New York with him because he'd screwed up their plans by getting caught. Fearing he might lose her for good, he wanted to try one more time to reason with her stepfather and convince him selling made sense. He took the boat from Indigo to Horne just after dark. Everyone was out burning, so no one saw him come across and tie the boat on the main dock.

Lowe went straight to the Leigh's front door, where Ann answered.

"What on earth are you doing here?" she asked him.

"I've come to talk to Mr. Leigh," Lowe told her.

"Is this what I think it's about?"

"It is."

"Well, don't mess this up too," she said, stepping aside to let him in. Ann was just as mad as her sister was at him.

"You're just the man I wanted to see," Mr. Leigh said when Lowe entered the foyer.

"Mr. Leigh," Lowe said, his voice wavering. "I know you're angry about everything. But I'd like the chance to talk to you."

"Well, it so happens there's something I'd like to talk to you about, Mr. Lowe."

"Can we take the Jeep for a ride?" Lowe asked, watching Ann watching them from the other side of the room.

"Of course," Mr. Leigh said. "I'll meet you out back."

While he waited for Mr. Leigh to come outside, Lowe went into the barn through the side door and brought Ann's Jeep out to the parking area through the pasture gate. He was closing the gate when he saw Mr. Leigh come out the back door. Lowe drove Mr. Leigh through the dark woods. Mr. Leigh didn't say much on the ride, just listened to Lowe's sales pitch. He told him about the neighborhoods and the golf course and how now was the ideal time to sell. Then after the short ride, they stopped on the back end of the field where everyone had been burning only minutes before. They didn't see anyone and figured everyone had packed in for the night.

Only when they'd gotten out of the Jeep and were standing there watching the smoldering ground did Mr. Leigh say he didn't want to hear anymore talk about selling the island.

"That all sounds fine, Lowe, and even reasonable. But my problem is that even if I were interested in selling Horne Island—I'm not—but even if I were, you are not a man I would do business with."

"But, sir," Lowe said, "You have a right to be mad, but Ann and Zada just wanted to come to you with a full plan. They wanted me to do all the work ahead of time, so you didn't have to worry about it."

"Sneaking behind my back on the development plans was the wrong way to go about it; but that's not what I'm talking about."

Mr. Leigh didn't continue because they saw a pair of headlights flick on from just down the road. An engine kicked on and the vehicle—Mr. Leigh's Jeep, it turned out—pulled up and parked near them. Ann got out.

"What are you doing here?" Lowe asked her.

"Oh, you know what I'm doing here. I should be a part of whatever conversation you are having."

"You followed us?" Mr. Leigh asked.

"Yes, I've been following you since you left the house. I had the lights off and stayed behind so you wouldn't see me."

"Well," Leigh said, "then you're just in time. I was just telling Mr. Lowe that I would never do business with him because he set me up with the game warden."

Ann and Lowe looked at each other and then back at Mr. Leigh. They didn't know he'd figured that out too.

"Now, Mr. Leigh, just give me a minute to explain," Lowe said.

"You made me look like a damn fool!" Mr. Leigh's face flushed red with anger. He looked Ann, and he must have seen guilt in her eyes. "And you were in on it, weren't you?"

She looked down at her feet.

"Well," Leigh said. "Lowe, I want you off Horne and Indigo for good. In fact, I never want to see you again. And Ann, you will repay me every cent I paid in fines and for the inconveniences of my friends with your Manhattan apartment."

"What? You can't sell my apartment!" she shrieked.

"I absolutely can. You can live on Horne with your mother and I."

"Oh, no. I refuse to live in Riverside Village. I am a grown woman—not a child."

"Well, unless you get a job or a husband to pay your rent somewhere, you'll live where I tell you."

Lowe says he could almost see the rage rise up and explode out of Ann. She surged toward her stepfather and planted both hands square in the old man's chest, pushing him with all her energy. The blow was solid, startling in its force even to Ann, and knocked her stepfather stumbling backwards. He lost his footing and fell like an oak through the air, landing with a heavy thump.

Ann and Lowe immediately rushed to help him back up. But as they knelt by his side, they realized his head had landed on a large masonry stone embedded in the ground. Blood pooled around his head and he wasn't moving. Lowe pressed his hand against Mr. Leigh's neck and couldn't find a pulse. The blow killed him.

They both panicked. They argued about what to do, but knowing the recent events suggested motive, they decided to try and cover up any evidence that they'd been there. Forensic investigations could detect hair follicles and skin cells on fabrics, and who knew what else they could find on a body. They did a shoddy job—not thinking about the Jeep tracks. And Roy's whistle must have fallen from a pocket on the coat she'd grabbed in her rush to follow them.

"It was stupid," Lowe says. "But neither one of us was thinking straight."

Once they got the body pulled into the fire, where they hoped it would burn up any forensic evidence linking the two of them to it, they decided to leave Mr. Leigh's Jeep so it looked like he drove it out. And they took Ann's Jeep back to the house. By now it was nearing midnight and all the lights in the houses had gone dark. Lowe, knowing he wasn't welcome already, wanted to be long-gone before anyone woke up, so he dropped Ann back at the house and, at her insistence, took the Jeep over on the barge in the middle of the night.

"So Ann must have left the pasture gate open when she came back in," I say, absorbing Lowe's story.

"Is that why she jumped?" Zada says, looking pained and confused. Then the coast guard boat comes speeding up to us. Men in black wetsuits and fins spring from the large vessel before it even stops moving. They move with choreographed efficiency. The uniformed captain on the boat and Doug exchange words—they want us to get away from the scene so we don't impede rescue efforts. Doug reluctantly starts the boat and drives slowly the rest of the way to the dock. No one looks away from the coast guard working in the river, except for Wilma. She nearly jumps off our boat before Doug docks it.

"My son is free," she howls, stumbling onto shore. "My son is free."

Howard helps Doug tie the boat while everyone disembarks. Detective Reynolds offers me his hand and hoists me up onto the dock. Then he stops Lowe, who was behind me.

"Mr. Steven Lowe," the detective says.

"Yes, sir."

"We need to take you to the station for questioning."

"I can explain everything," Lowe says as the uniformed officers flank him. Almost as if on cue, the wind dies. The officers guide Lowe into the back of the police cruiser. Zada, stunned, says little to anyone. But she follows the officers and Lowe out in Ann's Jeep. As the police leave and the marine rescue teams arrive, everyone's attention turns to what's happening on the water. I notice Howard standing alone on the dock and walk out to join him.

"What in the world happened out there?" he asks when I link my arm in his.

"I'm not sure I know exactly," I say. "But I do know this: things aren't always as they seem."

Epilogue

THE STORY OF HORNE ISLAND DOES HAVE A HAPPY ending, or at least mostly happy. Ann's body became entangled on a crab pot line not too far down the river from where she jumped overboard. When the tide went out, some locals were coming into the boat launch and saw her muddy limp body rolling against the riverbank. What sort of demons haunted that poor woman, I'll never know, and it was unfortunate that she came to such an end. But Roy and Wilma got to stay on Horne. Steven Lowe, although I never thought it would be possible, redeemed himself by finding an owner who wanted to preserve Horne. The new owner, who owned another historic plantation nearby, was easily convinced to keep Roy and Wilma on in their same positions. Tony, who'd recovered by then from his heart attack, but perhaps not his loss of PJ, was staying on the island to manage the transition. So the island wasn't lost to those who needed it the most.

With Mrs. Leigh gone and Tony back to managing the place, Howard and I didn't have much business on Horne anymore. But we did get to go on one last hunt.

I spent the whole afternoon in a tree stand without seeing a single deer until late in the afternoon. A cool breeze was blowing in a misty fog so heavy it almost felt like a light rain. By then I had all but stopped looking for deer because I knew I'd hear Howard's whistle any minute.

I was sitting there, listening to the woods, thinking about how grateful I was that the woods still existed, when I heard a snort from nearby. I slowly turned my head downward and saw a buck making tracks in my direction. My reverie broken, I became aware of my surroundings and fidgeted to get a firm grip on my gun. Then just as I was taking aim, I heard Howard's whistle and a rustle of footsteps moving through the underbrush. In a second, Howard and Roy were visible. The buck saw them too and darted out right past them. I groaned and collected my things to climb down from the stand.

"Did you see that deer?" Roy asked.

"She was probably sleeping on her gun," Howard joked.

"I had him until you scared him away."

Roy laughed and took my gun. Then we walked out to the Evening Trail where everyone else had already started gathering around the wagons. Rooster and John had gone in early (we all know why), and Tony hadn't hunted since his heart attack. But PJ was there. We'd left the girls at the house with Toot, where they were no doubt giving him trouble. And Steven Lowe, the city slicker outdoorsman, was seated at the top of the wagon like he was going to drive it in. He and Zada had been living on Indigo, which the Leigh's didn't sell, but they were leaving in the morning for Paris. When everyone was loaded into the wagon and situated in the seats, Roy jumped up and bumped Lowe out of the drivers seat. He flicked the reigns and the wagon lurched forward.

The fog thickened in the forest around the trail and the sky darkened above us. Howard and I sat together in the back of the wagon, riding to the big house just like the old days on the Evening Trail. I took a deep breath and tried to savor every moment of the ride. When we pulled around and the creek came into view, Howard nudged me and smiled.

"It will be cold on the boat ride home," he said.

I nodded. "And dark."

Then, at the same time, we both murmured, "What will the river reveal tonight?"

Duck Breast in Butter

Marinate the duck breast overnight in a robust red wine (i.e. a cabernet sauvignon).

Melt a liberal amount of butter in a frying pan, making sure it is hot enough to sear the meat but not burn butter.

Sear the meat quickly on both sides.

Add red currant jelly and red wine to pan.

Cook duck breast for approximately 3 minutes on each side, basting breast and stirring sauce.

The meat will be pink throughout.

Serve with wild rice and, pan sauce, and buttermilk cornbread.

Buttermilk Cornbread

½ cup butter

1 cup buttermilk

½ teaspoon baking powder

2/3 cup white sugar

1 cup cornmeal

2 eggs

1 cup all-purpose flour

½ teaspoon salt

Melt butter, stir in sugar and eggs, and beat until blended.

Combine buttermilk with baking soda and mix with egg mixture, and then add remaining ingredients. Batter may be a little lumpy.

Bake at 375 degrees in a greased 8-inch square pan for 40 minutes.